Level Zero

THE NEXTWORLD SERIES
BOOK ONE
JARON LEE KNUTH

SEVERED PRESS
HOBART TASMANIA

level zero

Copyright © 2011 Jaron Lee Knuth
Cover copyright © 2017 Severed Press

WWW.SEVEREDPRESS.COM

All rights reserved. No part of this book may be reproduced or transmitted in any form or by any electronic or mechanical means, including photocopying, recording or by any information and retrieval system, without the written permission of the publisher and author, except where permitted by law. This novel is a work of fiction. Names, characters, places and incidents are the product of the author's imagination, or are used fictitiously. Any resemblance to actual events, locales or persons, living or dead, is purely coincidental.

ISBN: 978-1-925597-70-7

All rights reserved.

Also by Jaron Lee Knuth

After Life
Fixing Sam
Demigod
The Infinite Life of Emily Crane
Nottingham

The NextWorld Series

Level Zero
Spawn Point
End Code

The Super Power Saga

Super Powers of Mass Destruction
Rise of the Supervillains
Fear the Empire

"Je pense, donc je suis."

- René Descartes

00000001

I hate the real world.

In the real world I'm a fifteen-year-old with pencil-thin arms that can barely lift my own acne-marked body, but in the virtual reality of NextWorld, my avatar looks like an old-west cowboy and my name is Arkade. I've got a dark tan and a five o'clock shadow covering the squarest jaw I could design. My arms are muscular. My chest is wide. My eyes are a steel blue that look out from under my wide-brimmed cowboy hat with a piercing glare. I'm awesome.

Everything is better in NextWorld. It offers a virtual domain for every kind of person, no matter how unique. There's DOTkid for the adolescents and babies that want to play with colorful dinosaurs and run around on rainbow roads. DOTedu is where the government forces me to spend at least six hours a day learning about authorized facts. DOTsoc has an infinite number of dance clubs, concerts, and social gatherings for even the most specific of interests. DOTcom is full of shopping districts offering all the digital products you might need: clothes, vehicles, or even real estate. But it's also home to all the auction houses and flea markets that sell used digital items of all kinds. DOTorg is a "free" domain designed like an outdoor park. Originally intended for family reunions, parties, or just a gathering place for the public, it ended up being an open forum for the disenfranchised to complain about their insignificant troubles. DOTnet houses the infrastructure of NextWorld, but the sewers of this domain are also where the hackers and illegal traders tend to hang out, in abandoned connections that not even the all-seeing, all-knowing DOTgov can watch. And do I even need to explain what goes on in the shadows of DOTxxx?

The domain I spend all of my time in is DOTfun, where all the online games exist, offering race tracks, flight simulators, combat battlefields, role-playing games, puzzle boards, and sports arenas of every kind. I play them all, but my current favorite is *DangerWar*. I'm good. I'm really good. It's not like my Player-Character name is in the top ten on the *DangerWar* scoreboard, but I've got close to one million kills, which just proves how much time I spend logged-in.

Tonight I'm playing the "Haunted Mansion" map in *DangerWar*, one of a hundred different scenarios. I've already killed fifteen players, and according to the scoreboard, there's only six left. Most of the players I've seen so far have been stumbling around the map, hoping and praying that wild swings of their swords and spraying bullets from their guns might manage to kill another player through sheer luck.

It's an easy night for me.

Flames crackle in a stone fireplace, filling the haunted mansion's library with an orange glow. Above the mantle, a painting of a decaying man watches my every move with eyes that follow me. As I step around the books that eerily float across the room from one bookshelf to another, I hear two different battles happening. The rattle of gunfire seeps through the floorboards below me, and the clanging sounds of a sword fight come from the room next to me. I check my ammunition and smile when I see plenty of rounds left in my shotgun. When I stop and pay attention to the different sounds of each gunshot, I can tell it's coming from four different guns. Two groups of players are firing from protected cover and wasting ammo.

I hate groups. I always play solo. I've never trusted other players, and I have no time for small talk with some little kid who doesn't even know how to play.

I press my boot on the floor and feel the weak boards bend under my weight. I reach into the satchel on my hip and dig out one of my plastic explosives. The item is expensive, but if I can take out the four players in the room below me, the price will be well worth it.

The explosive adheres to the floor with a pink, gummy backing. I select a five-second timer and push the green, flashing button. As soon as the counter begins, I walk away from the bomb and toward the sounds of the apparent sword fight coming from the next room.

I step toward the doorway, but a tall man wearing a tightly buttoned suit is holding a silver platter and blocking the entrance. On the platter is a curled up cobra that might have startled me if I hadn't played this map a thousand times. I recognize the manservant as an NPC (a "Non-Player-Character" controlled by the game), so I shove the useless distraction to the side and look inside the room. Two players are swinging metal weapons at each other, taking turns blocking attacks. One of them designed their avatar like a classic ninja wearing a black gi and wielding a katana sword. The other has the body of a demon, complete with horns and a long pointed tail, and he's wielding a curved scythe. They both turn toward the doorway when they hear the plastic explosive blow up behind me. Four names appear in front of me, a red X scratching over the top of each one to acknowledge my kills.

"Sorry to interrupt your dance recital," I say, my teeth clenched around a single toothpick.

One shotgun round blasts the ninja in the chest. His body shatters into three-dimensional pixels, tiny cubes that sprinkle against the floor before dissolving into nothingness. The demon jumps to the side, throwing out a swarm of knives in my general direction as I pump another round into the chamber of my shotgun. I barely need to lean my head to the side in order to dodge the spinning blades. They stick into the wall behind me.

I release another blast from my gun, but it only splinters a wooden bench after the demon dives behind it. He pops his head up, trying to lure me into firing again so he can charge me while I reload, but I stand my ground. I sidestep to the right, keeping my back against the wall, circling the room so I can get a better angle on the player.

As I step around a purple velvet chair and place myself next to the NPC manservant, the demon leaps out, charging me with his scythe held high above his head. I grab the tall NPC and shove him toward the swinging blade. I watch his silver platter fall to the floor as the scythe cuts the NPC in half. I lift my shotgun and pull the trigger. The barrel is only inches from the demon's face when the blast disintegrates his body. As the game crosses out his name in front of me, I wonder what the death must have looked like from his point of view.

A booming voice announces, "Winner: Arkade."

The haunted mansion melts from my view, leaving my avatar floating in a smoky mist. Multiple flashing screens appear in front of me. I reach out and touch the statistics for the game, and the screen enlarges. The Koins awarded to me for winning drop out of the sky, and I hear the satisfying noise of them clanging against each other inside the treasure chest that represents my personal inventory. It isn't much, but the game items I need are inexpensive. I make do with very little.

If I were a better player, like those in the top ten, I could make a decent living selling Koins in one of the DOTcom auction houses. The less experienced players are willing to spend real world credit on in-game Koins so they can boost their character's inventory, but real world credit doesn't interest me, nor does helping other players cheat. As long as the government keeps giving me payment vouchers for being a student, and those vouchers keep my account active, I don't need anything from the real world. The thought of graduation, and the end of those vouchers, makes me cringe.

I reach out and touch the item shopping screen, ready to replenish my stock of ammunition and plastic explosives, but an alarm sounds.

"Feeding time reminder," a lovely woman's voice says into my ear.

I sigh with annoyance, but as soon as I hear the reminder, I feel my stomach growl. Some citizens can afford devices that funnel vitamin paste into their bodies and siphon any waste they excrete, eliminating any need to log out, allowing them to live inside NextWorld twenty-fours a day. The price for such a device is so astronomical that it's unrealistic for someone who lives solely off student vouchers, but that doesn't stop me from dreaming.

I gesture for the log-out controls and push the large green button that rises from the smoky mist. I feel that familiar static tingle in my brain and close my eyes. When I open them, I'm staring at the illuminated metal interior of my E-Womb.

00000010

"Wireless connection disengaged from your nanomachines," the digitized voice says, sounding neither male nor female.

I rub my eyes with the palm of my hands and let my pupils dilate. The spherical E-Womb opens on the side, letting in the cold air from my room. I struggle to lift my legs out of the door because I haven't used them in nearly six hours. My feet feel numb when they hit the floor's metal grating. Thankfully the nanomachines swimming inside my body hyper-activate my nerve endings, and the feeling returns to my muscles.

My room is in tower #7395453-2075, located in the northern part of Old Russia. It's the same size as every single civilian room in every other tower on the planet: fifteen square feet.

When I was younger, I used to live in a larger family unit, but when my mother died, the government split my father and I into two single units. My father lives in the same tower, but thirty floors above me.

In the wall of my unit, the doorway of my E-Womb opens up next to my sink. On the other side of the sink is my toilet, which I sit down on immediately. I lean over to the vitapaste dispenser and stick my finger in the small, silver hole. The red scanner inside of the hole talks to my nanomachines, and I wait for the light to turn green. The dispenser opens, offering me a tube of the gray goo, specifically designed with whatever nutrients my nanomachines say that I'm lacking. My tongue salivates as my toothless gums swish the salty, super-dense caloric paste around in my mouth.

As I finish on the toilet, a train rumbles past my room, shaking the entire tower. I open the shutters of my single window and turn off the artificial sunlight, peering out across the cityscape. Water falls from the sky in large, thick droplets, as it always does. The citizens call it rain, but we all know it's the sewage runoff from the upper levels. From the height of my room, I can't see the ground, but there's no earth to see anyway. The cables and wires that make up the network of NextWorld cover the dirt and pavement. All I can see from my window are the twinkling lights of a thousand other windows that speckle the outside of the surrounding towers and a web of tubes carrying trains and automated walkways that connect citizens to each other.

My father was a child during the time of transition. The population had grown to a point where the size of the Earth was no longer capable of containing them all. Stepping outside meant rubbing shoulders with hundreds of other citizens. People were choosing lives that allowed them to stay inside the ever-growing heights of the world's towers. We could no longer spread outward, so we spread upward. As humanity continued to decimate the planet with pollution and constant civil war, citizens began giving up on the promises that the global government made. Things were getting worse, and no one wanted to face what tomorrow might bring.

The introduction of NextWorld is still comically attributed to the genius of one man, then global presidential candidate Xiong Chang. While it's obvious his team of programmers and designers were the real creators of NextWorld, Chang took sole credit for the invention that gave humanity the hope it needed.

We've all seen the video-cast of his speech: "Much like a brightly burning candle, our world has reached the end of its wax. Citizens of Earth, I'm here to tell you that I am your candlemaker. NextWorld will give us a place to grow and flourish, where once again our children can play on hilltops of flowing green grass, under a blue, cloudless sky, with the warmth of the sun cheerfully beaming down upon their faces. NextWorld is a place where we can conduct our business, socialize with friends, and do all the things the old world no longer allows, and now we can do it all from the comfort and safety of our tower rooms. NextWorld is mankind's next step, and I'm offering to hold your hand while we make that step, together."

The face of NextWorld won the election that year by a landslide. Forty years later, Chang's global government is still running both the real world and NextWorld.

The year before Chang introduced NextWorld, the healthcare system had already injected every citizen on the planet with nanomachines programmed to combat everything from diseases to the effects of aging. The brilliance of the NextWorld technology relied on using a wireless connection to transmit new signals to those same nanomachines from a device he called an "E-Womb." The E-Womb commands the nanomachines to intercept the signals between our brain and body, altering them in order to change our perceptions. The E-Womb can tell our brain what our eyes are seeing, what our skin is feeling, or even what our tongue is tasting. It changes our reality on an internal level.

When the real world logged on to NextWorld, everything changed. Our economy skyrocketed under a single digital currency. Jobs popped up all over the simulated frontier, and the unemployment rate dropped to a thousandth of a percent. Citizens who desperately wanted to reinvent themselves as virtual avatars snatched up all kinds of digital items. This was a culture hungry to redefine itself. Young and old found a corner to call their own and the infinite-sized NextWorld offered them endless possibilities. Mankind had hope again in this new existence.

But sadly, for most of us, the real world is still necessary.

I feel a headache coming on, a headache that only exists in the real world. I'm not sure if it's the fluorescent lighting, or the filtered air, or some sort of mental block, but it never takes long to swell inside my head once I've logged-out from the E-Womb. I glance at my bed and consider taking a nap, but the reflective screen above the sink is blinking, letting me know I have messages waiting for me.

Glancing at my frail, naked body in the surface of the screen, I touch the small message icon in the corner with a number three next to it. The screen displays the pending messages: two from my father, whom I haven't spoken to face-to-face in nearly three years, and a third message from my one and only friend, Xen.

I met Xen when we were little kids and the DOTedu school system encouraged socializing. At that age, you didn't need a reason to be friends, you just decided one day that you were. But as we grew up, our lives drifted apart, and now I find our friendship more of a hassle than a reward. We barely talk. We exchange a brief communication every week or so, with nothing more than "How are you? I'm fine" to tide us over until the next encounter.

I select my father's messages first, hesitating over the delete option before succumbing to the subconscious parental pressure to open them. They're text-casts, which only someone my father's age would send.

"Hi. It's your biological birthday next week. I know you don't care about these old rituals, but I need you to meet me in the communal area of our tower. My campaign team wants to hold a celebration for the news-casts. My re-election is coming up soon. I need this. Don't let me down."

I roll my eyes, deleting the message without considering a reply. The old man is a pretty well-known politician. He's only twenty-seven chairs underneath Global President Chang himself, which means nothing to me besides the constant harassment from him to "conduct myself like the son of a politician," whatever that means.

The birthday party is a joke. He tries to hold onto ideas that only existed before NextWorld. He likes to act like birthdays, religious holidays, and even family dinners are something that still matter, even though we'd just be squirting vitapaste into our mouths during awkward silences. It's all for show. He conducts all of his business in NextWorld. He campaigns in NextWorld. He wants to share my birthday party with the public via video-cast in NextWorld. Yet he acts like the real world is still some sacred place that should be respected.

I select the second message.

"Your mother would have wanted you to attend."

I delete this message even quicker. I don't want to hear about it. I don't want to think about it. I don't, and I can't. Not now.

I open Xen's video-cast before my thoughts lose me in their wickedness. The face of his avatar appears on the screen, standing in the middle of a dance club filled with avatars of every shape and size. Music throbs in the background, muffled by the background noise filter. Streams of color wash over Xen's avatar like liquid light. Xen designed his avatar with skin so pale it's almost translucent. His frame looks emaciated, like he's fasted his whole life. He's wearing loose orange wrappings like a Tibetan monk from a martial arts video-cast. He's yelling into the camera.

"Kade! When you finally quit playing your game, meet me in DOTsoc as soon as you can. Please. I'm at a place called Cherub Rock. I need to talk to you. Just… give me a few minutes. That's all I'm asking."

His face disappears. The options to reply, delete, or archive the message scroll onto the screen. I press the delete button.

I sigh, stressed by the drama of the message. I was expecting the usual brief check-in, not some urgent request for me to drive all the way across NextWorld to a dance club I'll only find irritating. I can't ignore him because the system lets him know if I've watched his message. I run my hand across my head, trying to push away the feeling. Shooting shotguns into people is so much easier than this. I squirt another mouthful of vitapaste into my mouth and crawl back into my E-Womb.

The idea of going to DOTsoc doesn't excite me. At all. It's the most popular domain in NextWorld, a place where avatars come to socialize and meet new people. The dance clubs might be more interesting than the real communal areas of the towers, where only the oldest citizens choose to congregate, but I've never understood the appeal of gyrating my avatar against the avatar of someone else while deafening music pounds into my ears and I hand over all my vouchers for liquid downloads that mess with my perceptions.

Xen acts like he would rather find a private room to meditate with a special group of people, or debate philosophy in the DOTgod domain, but he loves music. It's the only thing he loves as much as his weird religious beliefs, and he'll go to any shady corner of DOTsoc in order to hear his favorite bands.

I try to come up with an excuse, something to send him in a video-cast to let him know, "I sure wish I could meet you, but unfortunately..." Except he knows I have no life. He knows there's nothing going on except games, games, and more games. There's nowhere I "have" to be, because for me there's nothing about socializing with other people that feels anywhere near attractive.

I've known since a young age that there was something different about me, and that difference makes it impossible to relate to other people. Where I see only logic and rationale, emotions and romanticized ideals consume the lives of everyone else. I can't understand them, and they can't understand me, so I do us a both a favor and stay away. Yet here I am, about to meet my friend at a club full of dancing avatars who desperately want to talk to each other, because I can't come up with a good enough lie.

I close the door of my E-Womb and the inside of the sphere illuminates. I hear the hum of the machine. I feel the heat of the electricity wrap around me like a web of static. I curl up in the very center of the sphere, closing my eyes and letting the smallest smile form across my cheeks. I feel embraced.

I speak my two favorite words: "Log in."

00000011

My chosen spawn point is in front of the gates to the *DangerWar* lobby. As soon as my avatar appears, I'm gesturing in the air to open my inventory screen. I have a few options for traveling to the DOTsoc domain, but the only real choice is my one and only vehicle. High speed teleportation is too expensive. The bandwidth needed to move across domains instantaneously is something the government decided to charge for during the beta testing of NextWorld when they found too many avatars with short attention spans constantly teleported between random domains. The servers couldn't handle the onslaught. Besides, the sale of vehicles is yet another source of income for NextWorld, of which the government is more than happy to take their cut.

My vehicle started as a trashy, default car from a discount bin in DOTcom, but I picked it up in an auction house from someone who just wanted to delete the item from their inventory. It ran with horrendous lag, and its software was threatening to corrupt at any moment. I worked on it for nearly a year, forcing myself to use the public transit systems to get between domains until I got it running. But I didn't stop at simply making it work. I cranked out the baud rate so that it could scream through lines of code, chewing up virtual pavement like an extinct carnivore. I tweaked the image so that instead of a four-door family carrier, it became one giant wheel with extra knobby tread and a single seat where its axle should be.

When I select the wheel, the tiny representation grows, breaking from the confines of my inventory screen and landing hard on the ground next to me. I climb up into the seat and lean back, wrapping my hands around the controls. The wheel roars to life, emitting the preselected sound clip I designed: a combination of a jet engine and a prehistoric monster from an old animated video-cast. With a gentle push, the wheel bursts from the domain, tearing into the river of traffic that rushes around DOTfun. Most of the vehicles here are newer rides, designed by kids my age, but some are old hand-me-downs from their parents. It's late evening, so traffic jams clog the bandwidth near the entrance to the more popular games. My wheel is crawling at only thirty to forty petabytes per second. I pull onto a side street and make my way toward the domain's exit.

Once I'm outside DOTfun, I crank back the throttle, raising my speed to seventy exabytes per second. I lose myself in the thousand-lane super-highway that connects all of NextWorld. The road rises above all the domains. From my point of view I can see DOTcom rolling far below. The hypnotizing flash of blinking advertisements create a psychedelic display of colors and images. Bikini-clad nymphs holding virtual items, muscle-bound barbarians wearing virtual clothes, and avatar celebrities endorsing their favorite virtual locations. Every ad is selectable to give me more information and ordering options, even from this distance. My pop-up blocker is working overtime.

I pass by hundreds of different vehicles, each one as expressive of the user as their avatar. Most users choose to drive something modeled after real world vehicles from a bygone era: Convertibles, sport utility vehicles, roadsters, and chopper-style motorcycles. But then there are the more creative drivers, those with either enough money to hire a vehicle designer, or the education to build one themselves. These lucky individuals can travel NextWorld in anything from a mechanical spider, to a rocket-powered elephant on roller skates.

Some users can afford flying vehicles, which are able to take advantage of their own data streams, bypassing the conventional paths that NextWorld forces the middle class to use. I see a few of these fliers above the highway, amongst the NPC birds. They're nothing but tiny black dots against the default, cloudless blue sky of NextWorld. Inside the domains there are endless choices of environments, but out here in the connecting lanes, Global President Xiong Chang is the painter.

Past the birds, thousands of virtual feet above the surface of NextWorld, like a chrome moon in the sky, I see the metallic sheen of the DOTgov domain, with its single red flashing light. It looks tiny from this distance, but I'm well aware of the true size of the steel-plated globe that hangs above us all.

The traffic begins to slow when I reach the center of DOTcom. The congestion is eating up the bandwidth and everyone's vehicles slow down again. It takes me fifteen minutes to arrive in DOTsoc. Once I roll down the exit ramp, I make a left toward the club scene of the domain. DOTsoc offers lots of socializing experiences, from art museums, to gondola rides in re-creations of Old Europe, or beaches on the surface of alien planets, and hot air balloon rides underwater. I plug in the club name "Cherub Rock" and let the guidance system direct me through the domain. I glance down at the club's description.

CHERUB ROCK

An angelic experience for NextWorld citizens, creating an atmosphere of transcendence for you to center your inner chi and reach the next level of true virtual enlightenment in the safety of a non-PvP environment.

Tonight Only: The Fallen Sixwings will be ripping through their greatest Thrash-Mandala hits for your ears and soul to feel with our state-of-the-art audio-cast!

None of this surprises me. The post-neo-age religious nonsense sounds like the kind of thing Xen would attend. His parents raised him as an Omniversalist, and they were quite strict about their son's beliefs. But unlike a lot of teenagers, Xen never rebelled against the church. He embraces the teachings of the all-encompassing philosophy and never shuts up about it. It affects everything about him. The way his avatar looks. The way he talks to people. Even the voice he uses. Most kids his age speak with some version of new Mandarin, but Xen just repeats verses from the Omniversalism guidebook. Sometimes it feels like talking to a badly programmed NPC.

Cherub Rock's lack of Player vs. Player attacks isn't surprising either. They've zoned more than eighty percent of NextWorld for non-PvP violence. Most people don't want to respawn across NextWorld just because some bored, juvenile delinquent decided to lop off their avatar's head with a battleaxe. Something like that is annoying, frustrating, and can seriously ruin a decent business meeting. But some people love the constant danger, the nervous twitches of anxiety, and the ability to show everyone else how tough their avatar is. Of course, unless you're in DOTfun, and specifically in a game that allows levels for your avatar, no one is any "faster" or "stronger" than anyone else. Regardless, people like to flex whatever they can.

00000100

My wheel churns down the darkened streets, enveloped in the eternal nighttime of DOTsoc's club scene. A dizzying assortment of structures line the streets, spreading into the skies in a thousand different directions. I pass crowds of avatars in queue for concerts and bars, waiting for their chance to enter. No one pays attention to each other, gesturing within their own system screens that are invisible to everyone else, lost in audio and video-casts with absent avatars. I pass by on the street unnoticed.

I stop in front of Cherub Rock, the NextWorld positioning system on my wheel blinking green as it recognizes my arrival. The designer of the dance club modeled it after an old Catholic cathedral floating on a billowing cloud of white puffiness, animated stained glass windows running up the steeples. Tiny baby angels fill the sky, swarming around the church. Every few seconds they spray handfuls of glitter onto the avatars waiting in the queue below them.

After I stop the engine, I push the button labeled "INV" on the wheel's controls, and the vehicle shrinks back into my inventory. I straighten my swirling trench coat, adjust the wide brim of my cowboy hat, and step toward the bouncer. He looks like a caveman, with shoulders three times as wide as my own. His arms reach the ground, knuckles resting on the sidewalk below him. The only thing not prehistoric about him is the tuxedo he's wearing. The blank stare in his eyes lets me know he's an NPC.

"Whatchyo name?" he asks, an unmoving wall of muscle that blocks the doorway.

"Arkade," I say, tipping my hat.

A clipboard appears in his hand, and I roll my eyes at the lazy coding. He should have been holding it this whole time, or he could have pulled it from his suit jacket, but instead the programmer took a shortcut.

"Yur on da list," he says as he steps to the side.

I smile and try to ignore the line of glitter-covered avatars that groan with an impatient annoyance as they continue their wait. Every one of them has an avatar designed with minimal original designs. Most of them are right off the rack, with a slight change in hair color or a single piece of paid clothing. Even the few of them that have original designs are still uncreative and dull. I roll my eyes at them without realizing I'm playing the part of the snobby club goer.

When I pass through the front doors, the moderately-sized cathedral opens into a gigantic space that defies the laws of physics. The inside is bigger than the outside, a common trick with digital real estate developers. A stage floats above the center of the dance floor, holding the band so that they can see over the entire club. The singer's avatar has three heads, each singing into their own microphone, harmonizing perfectly. The drummer has eight arms. The third member has a rhythm guitar for her left arm, and a bass guitar for her right, both of them shooting lightning from the neck, each strike jumping to another of the random avatars that are dancing on every inch of floor, wall, and ceiling.

The gyrating horde is throbbing like one complete living entity with a thousand different heads. Each avatar has a tiny, selectable icon floating over them, which would give me access to their social screen, telling me everything from whether or not they were in a partnership, to what their favorite video-casts are, to pictures of their virtual pets. It makes meeting people easier, but it also makes it more apparent how few people I want to get to know.

The liquid light I saw in Xen's video-cast is still active, washing over everyone and leaving a rainbow effect that drips off their bodies. Thankfully, the owners of the club keep the temperature at a perfect degree for every avatar. The more you dance, the cooler it gets and the more comfortable you become. But the lights are flashing to the beat of the music, and the speed of the strobe effect makes me sick.

I step past an NPC waiter as an avatar shatters a bottle of virtual beer over his head. A few avatars scream, but most of them applaud the action and then return to their conversations. The virtual violence doesn't shock me. I've seen worse and far more often in DOTfun. Just because there's no PvP allowed, doesn't mean you can't have some fun with the virtual intelligence of the NPCs. NextWorld allows violence against NPCs everywhere. They just reboot and continue their programmed operations. No harm in that.

As I make my way toward the edge of the dance floor to look for Xen, I pass through the section of the club filled with tables. Groups of avatars huddle around them. It's easy to section off the cliques when they group together, their individuality becoming less apparent when surrounded by mirror-images of themselves.

As I'm thinking about the fact that even in DOTsoc I would prefer to play solo, Xen comes bursting through a group of scantily-clad cat people.

"Kade! Finally!"

He's screaming into my ear as his frail arms scoop me up, lifting me off the floor—an action that isn't normally allowed in a non-PvP environment. There must be something special written into the club's coding. When I look around and see numerous avatars rubbing against each other on the dance floor, I understand the need for the exception.

When Xen sets me down, I motion toward the bar, uncomfortable in the center of the dancing mass. He nods, and I follow his kung fu monk avatar toward the crowd swarming around the bartenders. Xen's arms separate the avatars, creating a walkway for me behind him. No one argues. Everyone knows Xen here.

When a golden-skinned NPC bartender approaches him, Xen looks back at me and asks me something, but I can't hear him. He makes a motion like he's drinking something, then lifts his hands as if to question me. I figure out his game of charades and shrug as if to say, "Whatever."

He grins at me, but it looks sneaky. He says something to the shiny bartender, who summons two billowing white drinks. Xen grabs both cups, letting the bartender deduct the price from his digital account of real world credit. He hands one of the cups to me.

I'm only fifteen in the real world. I'm still allowed access to virtual drinks and drugs in NextWorld, but until I reach that all important age of sixteen, there's a government imposed filter on the items I consume that negates their effect. Another archaic rule. Why should anyone restrict my actions in NextWorld based on how many years I've existed in the real world? I can feel the smoke I inhale entering my lungs, the pills going down my throat, and I can taste drinks that I swallow, but nothing has any kind of effect on my mind. I have no interest in messing with my perceptions, but it still bothers me that the decision isn't mine to make.

Xen has been sixteen for three months now, but I know he keeps his filter on as well. His Omniversalist teachings require him to remain sober. It makes the expense of the drinks even more of a waste, but his parents pay for all of his NextWorld transactions. They aren't rich, but they make good money cleaning air filtration tunnels in the real world, and have no use for NextWorld credit, so Xen can use as much as he wants. My father could afford to spoil me as well, but he tells me that living off student vouchers will encourage me to study harder and get a good job, because I'll know what it's like to live amongst the poverty class of NextWorld citizens.

I think he's just cheap.

Two stock avatars are standing next to us, draining large glasses of something and high-fiving each other. They both roar into the air, then throw their glasses at the bartender. The glasses shatter against the NPC's head, but no one notices. The two avatars laugh.

Xen looks disgusted, and I'm afraid he's about to start trouble. I've listened to his speeches enough times to know part of his religion—as ridiculous as it sounds—is treating all avatars, players and NPCs alike, with equal respect.

I grab his shoulder and say, "Let it go."

He replies, but the music is reaching its peak, with grinding noises and drumbeats so fast there's barely a space between each note. They all meld into each other.

"The music is too loud," I yell back, and select the subtitle option. "What did you say?"

He shakes his head and shouts, "I can't hear you. Private room?"

"Sure," I yell back, thankful to get away from the awkward social setting. "Invite me."

His frail arms gesture in the air, and I see him selecting a few options. He disappears, but seconds later an icon appears in front of me, alerting me to a room invitation from the only name in my contact list besides my father.

00000101

I select the icon and agree to the invitation. The club falls out of view like a two-dimensional curtain, fracturing into a pixelated version of itself as it drops. Behind the curtain is the virtual room, which becomes more defined as the club dissolves. Xen designed the circular room to appear like nothing but stars twinkling in space. The only solid ground is a floor made of multicolored pillows, like some sort of sultan's lounge. Xen's monk avatar is sitting in the middle of the room, leaning back and relaxing with a wooden mug in his hand. Steam and smoke pour from the mug like dry ice. He takes a long gulping pull off the drink, wipes his mouth, and then exhales loudly.

"Can I offer you a drink?" he asks, motioning toward the pillows on the floor.

"I'm fine," I say, awkwardly folding my legs underneath me as I sit.

"School got out nearly four hours ago. What've you been doing this whole time?"

My mouth opens, and I'm about to answer his question, when he stops me.

"Wait. Don't tell me. DOTfun."

I shrug.

"Don't you think those games are sort of a waste of time? You're not accomplishing anything in DOTfun."

"And in DOTsoc you're—"

"Interacting with humanity," he finishes for me. "Omniversalism teaches us that social interaction is what binds humanity together."

"I'm interacting. I just use guns instead of music."

"I interact with a different kind of humanity. Perhaps even a different *quality*."

His judgment annoys me and I roll my eyes. "All I see is quantity, not quality."

"They're all people, each with their own unique attributes to offer the world."

It's not even an argument. It's just more of his spiritual nonsense.

"Why not interact with people that are more like you?" I ask honestly, even though the tone of my voice makes it sound like I'm mocking him.

"And where would I find them?"

"DOTgod is full of people like you."

"Like me? No. Omniversalism teaches acceptance and understanding in order to foster peace, even in times of disagreement. With all the yelling and arguing, sometimes DOTgod can seem more violent than DOTfun."

I laugh. "Just admit that you'd rather listen to your favorite musicians than spend time in an actual church."

"Experiencing music makes me feel closer to God."

"Whatever," I say with a laugh, wiping my hand in the air to discard the conversation. "You wanted me here, and I'm here. So tell me what you wanted to tell me."

Xen's thin lips reveal the tiny set of teeth underneath when he smiles. "I met a girl."

I sit up straight. "Seriously? That's your big news? You meet girls every night."

"No, no, no. Not like this. This is different. I met her at a concert last night. Enchanted Saliva were playing at their own dedicated venue. The singer actually designed the place herself. It was amazing. Jungle themed, which I'll admit too many designers have overdone, but it had this sparkle to everything. Even the air. It made it feel... *ethereal*."

I give him a look.

He smiles. "That's what Raev called it. But she was right. It was the perfect word."

"Raev?"

"That's her name," he says, his eyes drifting off into space as he recollects the night, trying to find the right words to express himself. "She was dancing, but she wasn't using the default movements. She programmed this articulation to her avatar that I couldn't take my eyes off. And she was on this lily pad that was floating in this white water... like milk or something. But magical."

"Magic milk?"

"Exactly. I stopped watching the band and just watched her. I sat down in this super thick grass that had all these blinking fireflies that were swarming around me, and finally Raev noticed me staring at her—"

"Smooth."

"—and she smiled at me. And you know me. It's easy for me to talk to anyone. Girls included."

My voice is droll and monotone as I mumble, "I'm so happy for you. Really."

"But I sat there," he continues, as if he didn't hear me, "like I was still a little boy who gets sweaty and shaky when he gets around anything shaped like a girl."

"And that look worked for you?"

His eyes get big, and he looks even more excited when he says, "Exactly. That's *exactly* my point. It absolutely worked for me. That's how I knew that Raev was different. She came over, and she talked to me, and she had no idea who I was. My posturing and posing didn't affect her, yet *I* still impressed her. No. Wait. Impressed is the wrong word." He scratches his chin as he ponders his own vocabulary. Then he smiles when the word pops into his head. "I *intrigued* her. And Omniversalism teaches us to present ourselves in a way that's true and honest and... all the things that I was when I was with her."

"So you're telling me that you acted creepy, and she didn't run away? That's why you're excited?"

"Exactly. If that isn't love, then what is?"

I laugh. "Love? Seriously? Are you going to tell me you actually believe in that?"

"Is there a reason I shouldn't?"

"Because it's real world nonsense?"

"You're wrong, but I do understand why you'd say that. I used to think that too," Xen says, with a condescending smile, like he needs to speak more slowly for a confused child. "I used to think of the real world and NextWorld as two different places that exist next to each other. Which isn't the case. Raev explained it to me, and probably better than I can, but… the real world is out there." He waves his hand, pointing in no real direction. "And NextWorld… it's in here." He taps his head. "And in here." He pats his chest. "The real world is external, and NextWorld is internal. Does that make sense?"

I try to decide if he's joking or not. "Okay, Xen. Let's pretend everything you said isn't annoyingly poetic. What does any of that have to do with love?"

Xen's smile grows bigger as he says, "Everything. It has everything to do with love. Omniversalism teaches us that love is inside us… and that's where NextWorld resides."

I continue to stare.

"That makes it even more important, Kade. Love is even more important in NextWorld. And possibly even more powerful."

I rub my eyes, groaning loudly. "Did you really expect me to sit here and listen to this?"

"Honestly? No."

"Then why did you invite me here?"

"Because I was hoping our friendship might mean more to you than whatever it is that stops you from at least *respecting* my views."

"Oh great. Guilt."

Xen smiles with that knowing look in his eyes. "Do you think there might be a reason you feel guilty?"

"Why do I suddenly feel like I'm lying on a therapist's couch in DOTmed?"

Xen keeps a content look on his face, but his eyes won't lie. Someone designed them too realistically for that. My attitude disappoints him, with maybe a hint of anger as well, but he stays in the middle, always halfway between everything.

"Look, Xen, I'm happy for you. I really am. But I don't need to agree with every new philosophy you grab onto."

"I'm not asking you to."

"Then what are you asking me to do?"

Xen takes another deep pull off his mug, then exhales steam from his nostrils. He sets the mug down and folds his hands on his lap like he's about to meditate.

"I'd like you to come with me, to a concert, on Saturday night. I want you to meet Raev."

I exhale, but it comes out as a groan.

"What?" he says, with a snap.

"No. Nothing. I mean… who's the band?"

"Does it matter?"

"Not really."

"Kade, I'm being serious. I need this. I need you to do this. I need you to be a friend."

The guilt trip is twisting inside me. "Xen, this isn't fair."

"Fair?"

"Yes, fair. What you're trying to do right now. It isn't fair."

"What do you think I'm trying to do?"

"You're—"

"I'm asking you to be there for me. To meet this girl that I think I might love. That I *know* I love."

"Why? Why do you want this?"

He pauses, considering his reply.

I answer for him. "You're testing me, aren't you? Is this a test?"

"A test?"

"A test of my friendship."

"No. Omniversalism teaches us that if something is real, we don't need to test it or prove it. It simply needs to be."

"Of course it does. Look, I know I haven't been the best friend to you lately…"

"I'd hate to admit that's true, but I never see you anymore. This week I've only seen you at DOTedu, and they don't allow us to talk in class."

"I know."

"So come with me."

My brain is moving too slowly. I can't think of a viable reason to get out of going. I'm struggling, until I realize I can turn his guilt back on him.

"When was the last time you came to DOTfun with me?"

"When was the last time you asked?"

"That's not fair. I stopped asking because it became pointless to try."

His eyes shift back and forth as he tries to read me. My avatar is impeccable. I've spent way too much of my free time adding every detail I can to my face, which becomes a problem when I'm trying to hide something. He calls my bluff.

"Fine, Kade. Tomorrow night. I'll meet you in DOTfun after school. We can play whatever you want. Then you can come with me to the concert on Saturday."

"Um…"

"Great," he says, clapping his frail hands together, the tiny sound of the impact snaps inside the room. "It's a deal."

"Yeah. I mean—"

"This will be fun. I'm looking forward to it."

I try a last ditch effort to turn him off from the whole plan by saying, "I'm going to want to play *DangerWar*. It's violent. Really, really violent."

Xen shrugs and says, "I wouldn't expect anything else. I think that Omniversalism makes exceptions on virtual violence when someone is trying to reconnect with an old friend. I'll have to balance out my actions. I have a personal meditation room that I can—"

"Yeah. Of course you do."

"Yes. Of course I do."

I stand up from my chair and open an information screen, checking the time. I've wasted too many gaming minutes. I barely have enough time to shop and reload my inventory before I have to sleep. Class starts far too early.

I say goodbye to Xen, who's nothing but smiles. In fact, he's giddy. He excitedly tells me how much I'm going to love Raev, and how we're going to hit it off immediately and become best friends. He starts going into detail about the musicians she likes, the news-casts she follows, and her favorite video-casts. I act like I'm receiving an audio-cast from my father and log-out of the room.

I spend the entire drive back to DOTfun trying to come up with an excuse for Saturday. Nothing I think of seems believable, so I buy some plastic explosives, enough ammunition to kill a small nation, and curse my luck before disconnecting from my E-Womb. I fill up on vitapaste and crawl under the coarse blanket that covers my single bed. I try to sleep, but like every night, a train rumbles past my window every fifteen minutes, waking me from my already restless sleep.

00000110

Out of the central domains that make up the core of NextWorld, DOTedu is by far the most boring. It looks like a dull, gray facility that has no decorative design and only exists for a utilitarian function. It's also the smallest domain in NextWorld, at least on the exterior. The single building exists on a perfectly manicured lawn, with a NextWorld flag floating near the doorway. But this exterior is only an illusion, housing millions of classrooms inside the tiny structure.

You can see the punishing despair on the faces of the students in DOTedu. They may be laughing, talking, and chatting with friends in different screens, until they reach the gates to enter. Iron beams connect two brick supports, with a sign that reads: LEARN TODAY, FOR TOMORROW. The entire NextWorld community voted for the slogan, which barely beat: EDUCATE AND EXCEL.

Like every other student, I cringe when my wheel passes through the gate and the small schoolhouse blinks from my view. I know I'll be unable to log out until either my class ends or an authorized teacher grants me access to my E-Womb controls.

Much like the warden of a prison.

When my vision reappears, I only see the dull, neutral-colored walls of my first period class. My avatar changes to a default YOUNG-MALE-01 form, complete with a nondescript school uniform. The empty desks fill up with other identical avatars waiting for the bell to ring, but soon enough our teacher appears at the front of the room.

She's an NPC, and it shows. Her face looks lifeless, and her eyes are always staring straight forward. Her hair never moves. It looks more like one solid object than separate fibers. Her movements are stiff and robotic, programmed to appear natural by someone who apparently has no idea how humans actually move. Her voice puts emphasis in all the wrong places, which makes listening to her lectures a prolonged act of torture.

I hit the mute button and let the subtitles fall onto my notes, leaning back and letting my mind drift. I want to open a second screen and check the rankings of *DangerWar*, but DOTedu has my display locked down tight. I can only see one thing, and she's boring.

I don't think the boredom would bother me quite so much if I didn't constantly imagine what else DOTedu could be doing with the NextWorld interface. Here we are, sitting in a boring classroom designed to look like something from the last century of the real world, when we could be experiencing a virtual representation of any number of things first hand. We could be traveling through a human body for biology class, or watching historic battles happen right from the battlefield, or applying mathematics to physical actions, instead of hearing an unenthusiastic teacher tell us about these things as if we were still stuck in the real world. The limited imagination of the designers frustrates me to the point of anger. Someone gave them an endless amount of clay, and they decided to roll it into a ball. Brilliant.

I sit through six hours of "learning" before the bell sounds. I teleport my avatar out of the room before the last chime. My wheel is screaming down the super-highway, pushing my baud rate to its extreme with the thought of algebra and ancient civics only a fading memory. The congestion around DOTfun looks bad, and I consider logging out completely to let my avatar respawn in front of *DangerWar*, but it feels like too much work to face the cold of reality, so I open screens around me, checking my system for anything to distract me during the drive.

During class I received more text-casts from my father. My curiosity gets the better of me, and I open the first message.

"You're being immature. Send me a reply. You owe me that much."

I feel my blood pressure rise, and I close the message without reading the rest of it. I swipe my hand across his other text-casts, deleting them all with one gesture. Sometimes I wish they allowed kids my age to block their parents. It would make life a lot less stressful. I remind myself that I only need to wait a few more years, then I'll finally be an independent citizen in the real world and NextWorld. I'll only have to worry about my own actions. Like a true solo player.

I check the *DangerWar* scoreboard, and I see my name has dropped ten ranks, which causes a moment of slight panic. I take all the uncomfortable emotions I'm feeling and turn them forward, letting them push me into a dedication for the game that I can channel all weekend.

I skim through a few gamer news-casts while I wait for the onslaught of kids just released from DOTedu to funnel through the DOTfun gates, but as I'm about to close the display, I receive a video-cast. The blinking tag tells me that the sender has marked it urgent, but the name of the sender is a series of numbers. Since Xen is the only person on my contact list, I can't understand how it got through my spam filter. The fact that it's a video-cast makes me think it's an advertisement from DOTcom, something marketers like to call a "Commercial Experience." My logic tells me that I should delete the thing right away, for fear of some adware bogging down my bandwidth even more, or even worse, a hacker bypassing my security, but my boredom beats out my common sense. I touch the message and let the screen open directly in front of me.

A velvet blackness streams out of the screen, breaking the barrier and wrapping around me like a tunnel of ink. The music builds from the center, surrounding my head as the drumbeat reaches a crescendo and bursts into a deep bassline that I can feel in my chest.

"Congratulations," a voice says in a peaceful tone, yet with a dramatic excitement that eliminates the need to shout. "We are proud to announce your acceptance into the private beta test of NextWorld's most exciting new gaming experience."

Large letters made from rusted metal stream out from the center and spin around each other until they form a logo.

DANGERWAR 2

I hear the sound of an assault rifle spraying bullets, which shatter against the words. The letters retain their shape, even with the smoldering bullet holes. The announcer's voice becomes energetic as it recites the name. The music explodes, reaching its peak only to twinkle away into nothingness as the tunnel of black flashes a bright white light and disappears. All that remains is the title, floating in front of my face as I still sit in the center of my wheel, waiting in the queue to enter DOTfun.

"A brand new type of game, bringing with it everything players love about the original, and blending it with the most popular genres in DOTfun to create a single manifestation of fantasy violence like no one has ever experienced before. You will be among the first to witness the next step forward in both graphical realism and NPC intelligence. Welcome to the future of gaming. Welcome to *DangerWar 2*."

An avatar behind me yells from the turret of his tank. I shake my head and realize I've stopped driving forward. I'm stalling an entire lane of traffic. A warning flashes on my screen that I'm about to respawn at the back of the line if I don't keep moving, so I crank back on the throttle and roll my wheel through the gate.

I'm driving through DOTfun, but I'm unaware of my surroundings. The message I received is still open, the logo for *DangerWar 2* still floating in front of my eyes. I can't look away. I'm afraid that if I do, the logo will disappear and I'll realize that it was never real.

None of the news-casts have reported anything about a sequel being this far along in development, but we all knew it was coming. You don't make a game as lucrative as *DangerWar* without following it up with an even more ambitious sequel.

And now I get to test the beta version. I get to be one of the chosen few who sees the game first and makes sure it's perfect in every way, completely bug free, before they release it to the masses. My play time and my opinion will shape their game.

I'm not sure I could be any happier than at this very moment.

00000111

    My news-cast alerts pop up in multiple screens. Other permanent advertising screens placed around DOTfun change to show the breaking news. I'm not the only one who received an invitation and others have beat me to posting the information. Everyone is learning about the game at the same time.

    I pull my wheel over to the side of the road and watch the reaction of the population. The snarky commentary of players desperately trying to be cool by scoffing at the idea that a sequel could be anything but a pale impersonation of what made the original so unique quickly follows the initial amazement and excitement. Then comes the second wave of players trying to be extra snarky by mocking the first comments. It rolls into a flame war of nonsense until the general population is already forgetting about the news and continuing toward their destination. The mainstream hype dies within the span of a few minutes, yet I'm still sitting in the reclined seat of my wheel, staring at the floating logo in front of me.

    My twitching hand finally selects the logo. The letters explode, and a screen full of text opens up with pages of paragraphs. I start to scroll through them, but soon recognize the bulk of the message as an End-User License Agreement. I scroll through the law jargon until I find the question: "Do you agree?" I select the button marked "YES." It takes a moment, but the EULA eventually shatters, and a skeleton's head appears in front of me.

"Thank you for joining the private beta test of *DangerWar 2*. We thank you for your participation. Please make your way to the original *DangerWar* gate, and use one of these keys to gain entry."

The skeleton's mouth opens, and two stone keys roll out like a tongue. I grab the keys, and with a yank they pop free from his mouth and twirl out from my hand, landing in my inventory.

"Two keys?" I say out loud.

I don't expect a response from the automated NPC, but the preprogrammed explanation gives me one anyway. "We have awarded you with a second key for a guest. We specifically chose your user account because of your scoreboard ranking and/or the amount of time logged in to *DangerWar*, but we welcome you to bring any player with you, no matter his or her degree of experience."

I smile. Here Xen thought he was going to be playing the same old game that I always play, and I get to hand him the most coveted key in all of DOTfun. A part of me wants to rub it in his face that my end of our little social bargain outweighs his a thousand to one.

"Remember," the skeleton says, "we will disable all recording capabilities—video and audio—upon entering the game. We will also log all posts made by your avatar until the game's release to ensure your confidentiality about the game. Thank you for your cooperation, and have fun!"

The skeleton then cackles maniacally and shrinks until it disappears, which closes the video-cast. I pull my wheel back out into the stream of traffic and head directly for the *DangerWar* gate.

When I get there, a larger crowd than normal is hanging outside the entrance. The mainstream audience may have written off the announcement, but the real gamers are frothing at the mouth. I place my wheel in my inventory and make my way through the mob. A few avatars are standing on boxes, waving their spare keys in the air, encouraging the mass of avatars to bid on them, auction style. The other avatars—the ones who didn't receive keys—are waving different items for trade or holding up screens displaying their digital bank accounts. Some of the things they offer are shockingly expensive, worth way more than I expected people to part with just to join a beta test. NextWorld vehicles, real world E-Womb enhancements, even high-speed teleportation.

For a moment, I consider keeping my second key and auctioning it off for some nice avatar enhancements. I would accept any of those offers. I open my inventory and grab one of the keys, ready to hold it above my head, just as a tiny hand comes to rest on my shoulder.

"I could barely find you," Xen says from behind me. "I had to use the search function. This place is crazy."

"Yeah," I say sheepishly, and I fold the key into the palm of my hand, still unsure of what I'm going to do.

"I'm actually very excited!" Xen says with a big smile. "I know I give you a lot of grief for playing these games all the time, but Omniversalism teaches us to experience all that NextWorld has to offer, and it also teaches us to share those experiences with people we care about… so this is a very religious moment for me."

My eyes shift around at the rabid avatars, clamoring for the keys.

"So, how much do I need to spend to open a player account?" he asks.

"Well, uh…" I push the words out. "I have a surprise for you."

His eyes light up innocently. I hold up the key, and he looks at it with confusion. I walk him toward the gate as I explain what's happening with the crowd. I tell him about the message and why they chose me, and I even manage to not-so-subtly mention how much the keys are worth on the market. His reply is an attempt to hug me, but the domain blocks his avatar.

"Sorry," I say. "But if they let people touch each other out here, these avatars would be slaughtering each other trying to get at the keys."

"Of course," he says. "So, once we're inside the gate, what do I do? How does this work?"

"I don't know," I say, my voice squeaking a little with excitement. "That's the best part. This is a whole new game for me. It could be—" I stop to take a breath. "It could be *anything*."

When we reach the entrance, there's the normal entrance to the game, the forty-foot-tall arches, but then I see something brand new next to the monumental gate. A small, inconspicuous wooden door built into the wall. I feel my heart skip when I see it. I'm giddy with excitement as I jog toward it. The metal sign hanging from a single nail in the door has the number "2" etched onto it. I smile at Xen, then take another deep breath and slide my key through the small hole at the bottom of the doorknob.

I glance back at Xen, trying to wait for him, but he motions toward the door and says, "Just go."

I giggle and throw open the door, seeing only a strange black light beaming outward. I step through, and I hear the door slam shut behind me, leaving my avatar floating in the black of nothingness. I feel no ground beneath me, and I can see nothing but my own body. A familiar voice—that of the announcer from the original game—booms from the emptiness.

"Now loading: *DangerWar 2*."

00001000

The designers must not have the loading program completed because I can see the raw source code displayed in the blackness. Line after line of operations type out, with each letter standing as big as me. It types faster and faster until the words are almost falling out of the sky. It hits a line that says, "Load:player//run" and the screen flashes white, blinding me for a second.

When my pupils focus, I'm standing in a room made entirely of glass with a large glowing sign suspended in the air that reads: START. I look below me, through the glass floor, and I realize that the room is floating thousands of feet above a large city. As I study the architecture, I recognize the designs of the buildings from early twenty-first century video-casts. The skyscrapers are moderately sized, and look like Old North America. A jet fighter screams past my glass room, diving toward the buildings and rushing through the canyons created by the urban structures. A second jet chases after it. An ocean borders the eastern side of the city, full of ships with large billowing sails like something from a pirate-themed game. A desert stretches from the southern side of the city, and I can barely make out a single pyramid in the center of the otherwise empty dunes. A thick jungle grows right up to the western edge of the city, and I can see a few ruins poking above the tall foliage. Snow-capped mountains wrap around the northern side of the city. A medieval looking tower sits atop one of the tallest peaks, and I see a large, red, Japanese dragon flying in circles around it. I find the mixture of genres sort of strange, but the size and scope of the game's map amazes me. I wonder how far it stretches. Is there something on the other side of the ocean? Or is there anything on the other side of those mountains?

I look down at myself and notice something odd about my clothes. I switch to a third-person point of view and examine my avatar. I'm still the muscular male figure with the five o'clock shadow, and I'm still dressed in my cowboy hat and dusty Western clothing, but none of my extra gear exists. The trench coat I designed and the leather chaps covering my legs didn't offer my character any protection—*DangerWar* was a "one shot, one kill" type of game—but all that bulk looked cool, and I sort of miss it. I consider spending the time to design a new avatar, but I'm too excited to start the game.

I press the glowing start button in front of me.

"Choose your character class!" the announcer's voice says, vibrating the glass so much I'm afraid it might crack.

Two identical figures rise out of the floor. One has the word "Weapon User" printed on its chest. The other has the word "Magic User" printed on its chest.

This is nothing like the first *DangerWar*. There were no character classes and certainly no magic. Everyone's avatar held the same attributes. A player's skill and what weapons you chose to wield were the only things that affected your success. Of course they also confined the gameplay to small areas like haunted mansions, so I'm guessing I need to reevaluate everything I know about this game.

I hesitate, but eventually I choose what I'm comfortable playing. I touch the figure with "Weapon User" printed on its chest. Both figures explode into tiny shrapnel, none of which hits me, but all of which strikes the walls made of glass. Tiny spiderweb cracks spread out from the points of impact.

The announcer's voice booms inside the room again. "Choose your weapon!"

A ring of different implements of death hover in the air, spinning in a circle around me. I see swords, throwing knives, pistols, shotguns, bows, rocket launchers, axes, assault rifles, heavy machine guns, and some strange alien looking guns that look like nothing I've ever seen in any other game.

I've dabbled with enough of the fantasy role-playing game worlds in DOTfun to understand the importance of my choice. Not only will this be the weapon I start with, but depending on the rules, it may be the only weapon my avatar is able to wield.

The decision is hard. The biggest gun I see is the obvious choice, but I have no idea how this version of the game handles ammunition. If it's hard to come by, then the people wielding melee weapons might have a distinct advantage. I've been using a shotgun styled after the old West for the past year in the original *DangerWar*, but the maps are usually tighter, enclosed spaces. There's only a few maps that have wide open areas. Yet when I look below me, I can see far off into the distance and I think a sniper rifle sure could come in handy. Then I remember that I'm testing this game. In fact, my job is to break this game.

I take a deep breath and grab the pair of revolvers hovering next to each other. They can be a pain to reload, but they tend to make up for it in damage, and the fact that I can fire two at a time is even better. They feel good in my hands, like an old pair of gloves.

When I pull the guns from the ring of choices, the rest of the weapons explode, shattering the glass even further. The cracks spread out so much that it makes the walls nearly opaque. I take a step back and hear the glass floor crack under my weight.

"Now for your final choice."

I'm still holding the guns, examining the intense attention to detail from every angle, but the booming voice interrupts my gawking. Three words appear in front of me, glowing different colors.

Strength – Dexterity – Endurance

This is yet another option taken from the role-playing games of NextWorld. None of these choices are easy. None of them are bad options, but strength feels like it would be a waste. If I chose a sword or an ax, maybe it would affect my damage output. I consider dexterity, thinking it may help me fire faster, since other players will have automatic weapons. The contemplation drags on, and I'm getting antsy. I want to start playing, so I reach out and grab endurance. I'm hoping it will allow me to take more damage than other players. The word glows brighter and melds with my hand, filling my avatar with the same bright light. It fades a moment later, and the other two words explode. This time the explosion impacts the glass with such velocity that the entire room shatters into the open air.

I'm falling from thousands of feet above the city. The rooftops are rushing toward me, faster and faster as I reach terminal velocity. The air is whistling in my ears, the pressure is making my eyes water, and my breath escapes my lungs. I can't catch the scream that wants to release as I fall. My body tumbles in random directions as I'm wondering what I should be doing. This would be an obvious error in the coding if they spawn me into the game world from such an extreme height that my avatar dies when it hits the ground.

As I rush past the tallest skyscraper's peak, the building gives me context for how fast I'm falling. The windows are whipping past me so fast that they blur into a stream of glass. I roll around until I'm facing straight down at the pavement and watch it get closer and closer. I see people walking around, some of them stopping to look up and point at the falling man. I close my eyes because even though I know I'm not really falling toward the ground, and I'm not really going to hit the pavement, my brain is going to feel the pain. It will shock my system, and although it will only last for a split second, I will know what it feels like for the entirety of the split second, and I'm guessing it's not going to feel good. I squeeze my eyelids together, counting the seconds until impact and waiting for the inevitable respawn, hopefully somewhere closer to the ground this time.

Then the wind whistling in my ears becomes quieter. I feel the air that's blowing against my face become weaker. My eyes blink open, and although I still see the street coming near me, its approach is much slower. I float to the ground, and my feet touch down softly. As soon as I come to a stop, the announcer's voice booms through the city streets.

"Arkade has entered the game."

00001001

I'm expecting the crowd of people around me to attack me, but they look unarmed. They take note of me, then carry on with their business as if they have more important things to worry about than the man who fell from the sky. I'm wondering why none of them are attacking and why everyone's avatar is so dull. They're all wearing plain clothes, with fashion that matches the same era as the buildings.

I reach up and realize that during the entire fall my cowboy hat never fell off my head. I smile.

A horn honks behind me and I spin, yanking my revolvers out of the low-slung holsters hanging from my belt. I point the barrels in the direction of the noise, and I see a female avatar gripping the wheel of a car. I think that it's pretty cool they allow vehicles—which weren't a part of the original *DangerWar*—but I have no idea why the player honked her horn and stopped, instead of just running me over and letting her tires do the work. I don't wait to figure out her reasoning. I pull both triggers and fill the windshield with holes. The woman behind the wheel seizures, her body flopping in the seat as each bullet sinks into her chest. It only takes a second for her avatar to explode into useless pixels.

The other people on the sidewalk cower in fear behind mailboxes and parked cars. I point my guns, ready to open fire before one of them pulls a weapon from their inventory and catches me off guard. I don't understand why these players aren't attacking.

"Civilian NPCs are not worth any Koins," the announcer's voice says in my ear.

It takes me a second to register the warning.

"These avatars are NPCs?"

The announcer doesn't answer, but the possibility shocks me. The way they move and the graphics of their facial expressions seem too real to be artificial. Their reactions to my actions don't feel preprogrammed at all.

I step onto the curb and walk toward a woman coming out of a business with a sign that reads: "Nail Salon." She spots me nearing her, and a look of worry flashes across her face. I slide my revolvers back into their holsters and hold out both hands, showing her they're empty.

"I'm not going to hurt you," I say, and continue toward her.

Her eyes dart around to the other people on the street like she's waiting for someone else to tell her how to react. Everyone is watching me, frozen in place, waiting for any sudden movement on my part. I walk up close to her, but when I get within arm's reach, she steps back into the doorway.

"Stay back," she says. Her voice is shaking.

"Wow," I say, thinking out loud. "The coding skill needed to create that kind of emotional response is… it's incredible."

She looks confused. She keeps stepping away, backing into the nail salon. I keep following her, intrigued by her responses. I see fear. I see panic. I see her weighing her options. All of this is in her facial design. Most of the off-the-shelf player avatars don't even have this level of detail. When I follow her into the shop, the women who work in the salon yell at me, but it sounds like an old language, and I can't understand it. The fact that I can I see every variation in their skin tones—moles, wrinkles, and blemishes— exposes the hyper-detailed eye of the designers.

"I'm sorry," I say when one of the women yells louder, waving her hand in my face, still speaking in a language I don't recognize.

I shuffle my boots back out into the street and hear a rumbling like an avalanche of rocks tumbling down a hill. I turn around and see what has to be another player walking down the middle of the street. He's wearing baggy camouflage pants tucked into knee-high combat boots. His bare, tattooed arms are sticking out of an armored vest, and a gas mask from one of the earlier world wars covers his nose and mouth. Bright red dreadlocks sprout from the back of his head in a ponytail. He's straining his hands and bending his fingers in weird formations. Rocks float around him in swirling patterns, almost as if they were creating a protective barrier. The sound of the avalanche is coming from him.

He must be a magic user.

He doesn't seem to notice me, even though I'm standing out in the open, so I grab for my pistols and run sideways, strafing and firing as fast as I can. Every bullet I fire strikes one of the small rocks orbiting around him. I keep firing, but he keeps walking, ignoring me.

When he passes right in front of me, his head turns, glancing at me for a moment, and then I feel like someone stabs me in the back. The impact throws me to my knees. It feels like there's something sharp lodged between my shoulder blades. The pain is incredible, more realistic than the original game. My eyes water as the object digs deeper. I hear another rumble, and next to me the window of the nail salon—complete with the image of rainbow-colored fingernails—shatters. The NPCs on the street scream and scatter in every direction. I roll to the side as tiny rocks pelt the pavement all around me. I keep rolling, but I hear another rumble, and this time a long, sharpened rock, like a small stalagmite, pierces me in the chest. I can barely breathe. It feels like fire in my lungs and burning ash in my throat. The blood coming from the wound is warm. The game world turns red, and I can hear my own heartbeat in my ears. I should be freaking out, I'm dying after all, but instead I'm smiling ear to ear. This is all just so realistic. Even my death is impressively designed.

I drag myself behind the four-door sedan that I filled with bullets, which is still stalled in the center of the street. The game world around me looks like I'm trying to see through red liquid. It wobbles and waivers with the spinning feeling in my head. I see another long stalagmite shatter the side mirror on the car, right next to my head. I peek over the hood and see the man in the gas mask brazenly walking toward me, approaching the car as if he doesn't have a single worry.

I've only been in the game for five minutes and I'm already going to die.

"Sorry, kid," the magic user says, his voice sounding inhuman through the filter on the gas mask. "I'm only passing through the city zone, and I can't waste time with someone who doesn't even understand how to play the game."

And that's when he throws up one of his hands. I hear the rumble grow with intensity as a long pointed rock flies from his hand and strikes me right between the eyes. The game world goes black.

"Grael: Level 72, has killed you."

Level 72? No wonder he annihilated me, and no wonder I couldn't hit him. The extreme level gap should make me feel better about him slaughtering me like that, but it still frustrates me. In the original *DangerWar*, everyone was on the same playing field. There were no levels. I could be the best, because I was the most skilled player. It took a level 72 three shots to kill me. Two in the torso, one in the head. I take note of this and thank myself for choosing endurance as my view fades into existence again.

At least the sensation of pain cancels when I respawn. My avatar materializes outside of the game. I'm standing near the gates, right next to the door. A throng of spectators has gathered nearby and many of them are staring at me, waiting for my reaction. Another player flashes into view, standing almost shoulder to shoulder with me. He glances around, taking in his surroundings, disoriented from the respawn. As soon as he sees the crowd, he raises his hands in the air and says, "That was awesome!"

The crowd of avatars cheer. Many of them are newscasters, and they submit the new information to whatever news-cast employs them. The player next to me runs back for the door, disappearing as soon he steps through it.

A newscaster turns his video-cast toward me and asks, "Can you give us any information? Anything at all. What's it like inside *DangerWar 2*? What happened?"

"What happened?" I repeat his question before I clench my fists. "I died."

00001010

I watch NextWorld drop from my view as I pass through the *DangerWar 2* doorway. Instead of falling from the sky, this time I materialize in an alleyway. A civilian NPC with grease stains covering the belly of his apron is tossing a garbage bag into a dumpster. I hear the groan of a homeless man under a piece of cardboard by my feet. Water drips out of a pipe, creating a puddle on the pavement. The sun is setting below the horizon, giving the city a sort of orange glow.

"Welcome back to *DangerWar 2*," the announcer says.

I feel more secure and not so exposed, hidden between the two buildings. I lean my back against the wall and let myself think. I don't like feeling so weak, and that player, Grael, made me feel weak. How did he reach level 72 so fast? He must have been playing longer than anyone else, but how is that possible?

I touch the handles of my revolvers that are snug in the holsters hanging from my belt. I need to level up my character. I need Koins. But how do I get them? There was no tutorial. There was no explanation. I'm assuming that I need to hunt down and kill other players, a carryover from the original game.

Then I remember what the announcer said: "Civilian NPCs are not worth any Koins." Which means there might be NPCs that *are* worth something. That's good to know.

I gesture in the air, opening a few different screens. My inventory only contains my revolvers and the treasure chest for my awarded Koins. The map of the game world has a shaded area to show me where I've been and where I've yet to explore. My avatar profile shows that I'm level 1. It compares game statistics like how many times I've killed other players and how many times other players have killed me. I don't like seeing the "0-1" as my current rating.

The word "QUESTS" is at the top of the final screen. I frown. Another role-playing game idea. There was never any goal in the original *DangerWar* besides killing. It was simple. Clean. Pure.

I open the Quest screen, and a long piece of brittle parchment unrolls in front of me. Words begin to appear on the paper as if an invisible pen is writing them.

"Welcome to *DangerWar 2*. As one of our beta testers, we encourage you to find an equipment shop. There we will grant you your first opportunity to spend any Koins you may have accumulated and learn more about this brand new game world."

As soon as the quest writes the last word, the map screen opens and a flashing light appears in the shaded area, over the top of a building about fifteen blocks from where I'm standing. I swipe all the screens shut. I feel better. I know what to do. I have a purpose again.

I consider stepping back out into the streets, but I can still subconsciously feel the impact of the sharpened rock between my eyes. When I look up, I see a fire escape bolted to the side of the building. Being up high is a much better vantage point, so I leap up and climb the ladder that's hanging from the structure.

I rush up the stairs, past the windows with the glass missing and plywood nailed to the outside of the frame. When I reach the top, I'm able to see a few blocks in each direction. Taller buildings stop me from seeing any farther than that. I open the map of the city streets and re-size it so that it's floating in the lower right corner of my vision. I rush toward the next building and leap when I get to the edge. The distance my avatar can jump is unrealistic, just like in the original game, so I clear the alleyway easily. I stay on the rooftops for three blocks, leaping over the gaps between buildings and climbing fire escapes when I need to ascend higher.

As I jump across another alleyway, toward a five-story apartment complex, I hear gunfire coming from inside the structure. As I grab onto the metal walkway of the fire escape and climb onto the last platform, the window next to me breaks open and bullets zip past me. I slam up against the brick wall, yanking out my guns and listening for my attacker, but all I hear is more gunfire spewing from a fully-automatic rifle.

Just as I'm about to peek around the corner, I hear boots slapping against tile. A figure leaps from the window, dives through the air, and barely grabs onto the edge of the adjacent rooftop. I notice the assault rifle strapped to her back as her feet scramble against the wall, trying to lift herself onto the roof. I raise my guns, hoping for an easy kill, but just as I get the avatar in my sights, I hear a burst of air from the window next to me. Out of the corner of my eye I see a rocket fire from within the building and go whistling across the alleyway, striking the player clinging to the edge. The explosion is so close that I crouch down and cover my head, the sound deafening my ears for a few seconds. When I open my eyes, the entire wall of the building is crumbling around the disintegrated avatar.

Knowing that rocket launchers are notoriously slow to reload, I waste no time twirling around to peer inside the window. I see a robotic-looking avatar with a bazooka resting on his shoulder. He's so focused on congratulating himself on the kill that he doesn't notice me raise my pistols and pull the triggers. The bullets strike him in the chest, propelling him down the hallway. My choice of weapons pleases me.

The robot avatar drops his bazooka, and as his body slams into the far wall, I keep the barrels trained on him. When I see him move, I unleash a few more rounds, these bullets pounding into his head, leaving smoking holes in his metal skull. When his body drops to the ground, his avatar disintegrates into a spray of pixels.

"You have killed Robomojo: Level 2. You have earned 100 Koins."

I step through the window and into the hallway, destroyed by gunfire before I even arrived. I walk toward the rocket launcher that Robomojo dropped, but before I can pick it up to examine it, it disappears in the same pixelated spray as his avatar. That's disappointing. In the old version of *DangerWar*, it was always a good idea to grab whatever dropped gear I could find. If I wanted, I could trade it in for Koins at the end of the game, but any implements of death that I could scavenge off my fallen foes might come in handy later.

I open the cylinders on both of my pistols to reload them, but I find that they're still full of bullets. No reloading required? I'm suddenly even more happy with my choice of weapons and thanking my luck that Robomojo didn't fire another rocket as soon as I showed myself. I have to remember that I don't know anything about this game.

"Feeding time reminder," a lovely woman's voice says into my ear.

I've felt my stomach growling since I left DOTedu, but the excitement of the invitation made it easy to ignore. I open my basic NextWorld controls and disable the reminder. There's no way I'm stopping now. Not when I've barely scratched the surface of the game.

I check my map. The equipment shop is only two blocks away. Going back out on the street is dangerous, but I need to provide myself with as many opportunities to kill other players as possible. This, of course, means just as many opportunities for other players to kill me, but that's how you play the game.

As I'm running down the stairs of the apartment building, I realize I'm getting too caught up in the excitement. I'm making the mistakes of a brand new player. I should know better. The sound of combat always draws other players. I should have been moving away from the area or placing myself in an advantageous position as soon as the fighting stopped. I pay the price for my lapse in critical thinking when I reach the entryway of the apartment building. The front doors burst open, and I see hands toss two grenades into the air. Luckily my gamer-brain kicks in. I leap over the railing without thinking, dropping behind a vending machine on the side of the staircase as the grenades bounce across the floor and explode a second later. The metal vending machine takes the brunt of the blast.

My ears are ringing again. As the whine inside my head fades, I hear muffled shouting. The yelling isn't angry. It sounds like someone shouting directions. Two players are working together. I didn't know team play was possible. I need to find Xen. Or maybe that isn't a good idea. Maybe I should find someone more experienced with *DangerWar* or gaming in general.

I put the idea aside for now and keep myself hidden. When I see feet making their way up the stairs next to me, I point both pistols and fire them straight through the wooden steps. The wood is weak, and it only takes a few shots for the bullets to blast their way through the material. The shots hit the player that looks like a half-man/half-bulldog wearing a basketball jersey, and he tumbles back down the steps. The other player, a half-man/half-rottweiler, screams as he throws another grenade toward the steps. I dive to the right and the explosion misses me by inches. I keep squeezing the triggers of my own guns, waving the barrels toward him. The line of fire drags across the room, tearing apart the wallpaper and paintings on the far wall. I see him pull out yet another grenade, so I stop firing for a second and take the time to carefully aim my next shot. The single bullet strikes the grenade in his hand. The explosive drops, but the pin is still in the device. It rolls harmlessly across the carpet.

The bulldog-man that I initially struck climbs to his feet at the bottom of the stairs. I see him open his inventory with a gesture, and within half a second he's holding a chain-fed heavy machine gun in both hands. The chain of bullets streams out of the side of the weapon, flowing all the way to the floor. I try to spin quick enough, but I already see the bulldog-man smiling.

I run to my left before he fires. The gun pours out rounds like a hose of death. It tears apart the metal vending machine, and the stream of bullets chases me across the room. I keep running, but I can hear the destruction right behind every one of my steps, turning the wall into a cloud of splinters. I dive through an open door on the other side of the entryway. Behind me, the door folds under the impact of hundreds of bullets pounding against it.

The player finally lets up on the trigger, and I hear the last of the empty shell casings falling to the floor. He kicks the casings to the side as he walks toward the doorway. I crawl behind the desk in the room and hide underneath it. I can hear the two dog-men yelling at each other.

"Deka! You still with me?"

"He shot the grenade right out of my hands!" the other one calls out, his voice sounding whiny, like a little boy whose voice hasn't dropped. "His stupid pistols shouldn't be that powerful. How is that fair? It's not fair, at all. This game is stupid."

"Don't sweat it. It was a lucky shot. We're going to kill this guy, and we're going to use the Koins to beef up our weapons. Simple as that."

There's a pause, and the other player whimpers out, "Yeah. Okay. Fine."

I peek under the desk and see two pairs of sneakers step into the doorway and the chain of bullets drop to the floor.

"Come out, come out, wherever you are."

The high-pitched laugh of the bulldog-man is as annoying as when he speaks. I cringe when I think about how easy it's going to be for him to just toss a grenade into the room and write me off. Or the rottweiler-man's giant gun could just tear through the wooden desk like it's a stack of toothpicks. I could always try to pop up and shoot them both, but the only way I'd win that draw is if I got two head shots, and even then there's no guarantee they aren't endurance-enhanced like me. I'm angry that I got myself into a situation where I'm going to die again so quickly. I want to close my eyes and wait for the respawn, but I refuse to go down like that. I grip the pistols tight and tense my legs, ready to pop out from my hiding spot.

Before I can move, I hear an explosion and the sound of shocked screaming. I peek under the desk and see the two avatars fall to the floor, covered in green flames. They burn for a moment, but when the screaming stops, they dissipate into pixels. Seconds later I see skinny legs step through the doorway wearing the orange wrappings of a kung fu monk.

00001011

"Xen?" I whisper to myself as I poke my head up from underneath the desk.

He stands in the doorway holding balls of green flame in both hands. His arm reels back, ready to hurl the fire, but when his eyes focus in on me, a smile reveals his white teeth.

"Kade! What are you—"

I raise one pistol, ready to blast him while the sight of me is still disorienting him, but I see him lowering his flaming hands. He has no intention of attacking me. It would be an easy kill. I squeeze the trigger. The hammer inches backward.

I'm a solo player. I don't want to rely on anyone, least of all someone who doesn't know how to play the game. But do any of us know how to play this game? I may have a slight advantage, but the other players have almost killed me twice, and I only managed to kill one of them. Maybe solo play isn't possible. If anything, Xen will provide something else for the other players to aim at instead of me. I lower my gun and step up to him.

"Thanks for the assist," I say and hold out my hand.

He shakes it, and as soon as our palms touch, both a YES and a NO button appear in between us.

The announcer's voice asks, "Would you like to form a group?"

"Of course I would!" Xen says and hits the YES button.

I hesitate, but the situation feels awkward. I'm not sure what would happen if I pushed the NO button. I try to imagine Xen's reaction. The betrayal I picture in his eyes makes me uneasy. I lift my hand and touch the green YES button. A bright outline forms around Xen's monk avatar and a tiny dot appears on my map, signifying his location.

"This will be a lot more fun now," Xen says, "I wouldn't want to play this game alone. Omniversalism hasn't taught me much about how to kill people."

He laughs, but I try to ignore him, staying serious. I don't want to be friendly. I want to focus on the game.

"You need to be careful," I say. "We're going to be splitting Koins now. Your actions will affect my ratings."

The smile drifts from his face. "Right. Sorry."

I ignore his change in attitude and say, "I'm trying to get to an equipment shop. It's the first quest, so you should have it too."

Xen stares at me with a confused look on his face.

"Open your menu screen," I say.

Xen gestures in the air. I hear music start to play, a piano melody mixed with a saxophone. "Neat," he says. "I even have access to my music library."

"Shut it off. We need to focus on the game."

The music stops, and he continues to gesture.

"I didn't even know these menus were here. I've just been wandering around, killing players. How stupid am I?"

I cringe as I ask, "How many players have you killed?"

He thinks for a moment and says, "Only five. I just reached level 2."

I keep my own statistics to myself. No need to give Xen a big head. "We're going to have more players on us if we don't keep moving." I hold up my guns. "These things are powerful, but I wouldn't mind buying some upgrades."

His eyes bug out when he sees my weapon. "You're using pistols? Are they any good?"

I squint my eyes. "You'd be surprised."

He holds up his hand and green flames erupt from his palm. "I chose magic user. I never run out of ammo, but I throw fire sort of slowly. I had my choice of elements to wield, but I thought fire would be the best. I figured I could do the most damage with that. Damage is important, right?"

I roll my eyes and pretend I understand the rules better than I do. "Magic is like any other weapon. It's all about the person wielding it. If you're not a good player, it doesn't matter what element you choose."

"Oh," he says, trying to break past the awkwardness of my snippy comment. He smiles again and says, "I have to admit, Kade, this is pretty fun. I can see how you could lose yourself in something like this. It's a great way to express… pent-up aggression."

"The players that get too wrapped up in having fun are the ones that get killed. Stay focused."

His smile drifts away again. I feel bad, but I'm not here to entertain him. This is important to me. I can't worry about his feelings. I look at my map and reorient myself. I point toward the northeast.

"Let's get moving. I'll lead, but I need you to watch my back."

Xen hesitates for a moment. I can tell he wants to say something, but I try not to make eye contact. He nods, and we sneak out the front door of the building, crouching behind parked cars. The civilian NPCs are still walking through their programmed lives as if there isn't a war happening around them. We sprint across the street and duck behind a mailbox. Xen's hands are flaming as he looks both ways, keeping his eye out for anyone that looks suspicious. I tap his shoulder to let him know we should move—the entrance to the store is only a block away—just as something huge passes overhead. I notice the shadow before I look up and see a fighter jet flying low, streaking between the buildings. The roar of the engine follows behind it, shattering the windows it passes. NPCs run for cover as the shards of glass sprinkle across the pavement.

"They have jets in this game?" Xen asks, as if I should have an answer.

"Apparently. But I haven't seen any available in the starting zones. Maybe they're available at higher levels." I pause as I remember the magic user that killed me in the street. "Earlier I saw a player that was already level 72, which I still don't understand. How could anyone have reached that level so fast?"

Xen thinks for a second and says, "Maybe some players are older, people who have already graduated from DOTedu, and they were able to play while we were in class."

I consider the theory, but I have to rebuke it. "One afternoon still shouldn't be enough time to reach level 72."

Xen keeps staring into the sky. "I hope we can find an airplane. It looks like fun."

I want to smile. He's finally clicking in to what can be so fun about simulations. But I keep myself cold.

"Let's go."

I give him a nudge down the street. He nods over his shoulder and continues to sprint behind me, crouched down to make himself a smaller target. His skinny monk avatar is coming in handy. His bright orange wrappings, not so much.

Across the street from the marked objective on the map, we crouch behind an abandoned car that sits on cinder blocks. The building that houses the equipment shop looks empty, with windows that are boarded up and graffiti sprayed across the front door. I spot a neon sign hanging in the window that reads: OPEN.

I stand up to walk around the car, but Xen grabs onto my shirt and yanks me back down to the ground. I'm ready to let loose an outburst of anger, but I see him readying a handful of green fire and looking the other direction. I follow his gaze and see a military-style jeep turn the corner, moving at a crawl. The driver looks like a basic, muscle-bound soldier with camouflage paint streaked across his face. The avatar standing in the back of the jeep, manning the mounted gun, has a long lizard face and scaly skin. He's moving the gun back and forth, methodically scanning both sides of the street.

"Do we hide?" Xen asks, his hands twitching.

I look at the jeep and smile. "Hiding is boring. But try not to damage the vehicle. We need a ride."

I stand up and target the driver. Their slow movement makes it easy to bring him into my sights. With a single trigger pull, I release one bullet straight through the windshield and into the avatar's head.

The jeep wheels to the right, crashing into a streetlight. The lizard on the mounted gun braces himself, and as soon as the jeep comes to a harsh stop, he spins the barrel toward me. I duck back behind the hood as the gun pounds the abandoned car, puncturing the metal doors and shattering the windows. Xen leaps out from the back and tosses one of his fireballs. The blast hits the lizard in the shoulder, knocking him to the side. The player manages to maintain his grip on the gun, but the barrel goes spinning, spraying bullets across the street. I pop up from my hiding place, gripping one pistol with both hands and bracing my arms on the hood of the car. I give myself a few extra seconds to train my sights on the lizard as Xen continues to hurl fireballs. Just as I'm about the pull the trigger, bullets pepper the front of the car. I duck back behind cover and watch Xen do the same.

"The driver," Xen yells. "He's not dead."

I grit my teeth. I was sure a head shot would have dropped him. He must have chosen endurance like me. It might only give the players that choose it a few extras hits, but in a situation like this, it's priceless.

"I've got him," I say. "Throw out some fire to distract him."

Xen rolls to the back of the car and summons a ball of flame in his hands. He tosses it over the car without looking, and I hear gunfire hitting the trunk. I draw my other pistol and spin around the front of the car. I squeeze the triggers before I'm even aiming. The bullets are striking the wall above the driver's head, so I adjust my aim toward his chest. His body shakes as each bullet hits him until his avatar explodes into pixels. I see the lizard climbing back into the jeep, but before I can fire again, a ball of green flame strikes him between the shoulders.

"Your group has killed Sadistik: Level 3, and Skael: Level 2. You have earned five-hundred Koins." My avatar flashes brightly, and I hear the announcer say, "Welcome to level 2."

00001100

The door to the equipment shop hangs crookedly from one hinge, but when I look inside, the difference in quality is shocking. While the outside appears to be a dilapidated, four-story building, the inside looks like a small, single room with clean, steel walls and a holographic screen floating in the center. The rest of the room is completely empty.

When both Xen and I step inside, an armored door seals shut behind us, locking us into the protected room. The holographic screen lights up, showing the same skeletal face that awarded me the two beta keys.

"Hello," he says with a booming voice that I recognize as the announcer. "Thank you for taking place in the beta test of *DangerWar 2*. I sincerely hope you've already enjoyed your experience in our brand new game world. We want you to focus on having fun. We do not require you to file any error records or quality control reports. We do not require you to do anything but play the game as you normally would. Our teams are logging your every move, so any bugs that you may come across will be sent directly to them."

Without lips, the skeleton looks as if it's always smiling. "I hope you've already noticed the improvements we've created for you to enjoy. Beyond the obvious changes to the rule system and graphical upgrades, the game world of *DangerWar 2* itself has grown immensely. Instead of a series of small maps working independently, we decided to put all players into a single game world, connecting our different ideas into a giant, cohesive existence. We feel this will create a much more unified experience for players, as well as give everyone more opportunities to interact. Which brings us to the second major improvement."

The image of the skeleton grows larger, as if it's leaning in closer to the camera. "NPCs now play a much bigger role in the game world. Where the original *DangerWar* treated them as merely decorative pieces of the map, *DangerWar 2* has introduced an all new artificial intelligence that encourages them to play a much more significant role in your experience. Our team of programmers have spent years developing code that would replicate the most realistic of human actions. We hope the difference between combat with players and NPCs will be negligible."

I hear Xen say, "That's beautiful. Omniversalism teaches us the importance of recognizing the soul in every avatar."

I think about my confusion when I first landed in the street. I couldn't tell them apart, at least not at first.

"I'm sure you're excited to continue on your adventure, so I won't take up anymore of your time. You've succeeded in finding your first equipment shop, one of the few locations in the entire game world of *DangerWar 2* where you're completely safe. No enemies can enter or attack you when you're inside, and this is the only area that isn't zoned for PvP. Congratulations. Because of your arrival, you have completed your very first quest."

I hear the announcer's voice boom into my ear as it normally does. "Quest completed. You have earned 1,500 Koins." My body lights up again and the announcer adds, "Welcome to level 3."

The skull continues his toothy smile as it says, "You may use this screen to spend your Koins toward upgrades for your avatar. You may search for quests from your quest screen, but don't waste any time. Those same quests are available to all other players, so you want to complete them before anyone else does. There are many more surprises awaiting you in the world of *DangerWar 2*, and we hope you find them all! So? What are you waiting for? Get out there and play!"

The skull fades away, leaving a touch menu in its place. I look at Xen and excitement lights his eyes. He looks down at his own hands and clenches his fists.

"That was a lot of Koins for just finding this equipment shop," he says. "I'm level 3 now!"

"Me too," I say, trying to play it cool by feigning boredom with the idea, when in reality it couldn't excite me more. "It looks like quests are the way to earn the most Koins. The players out there are wasting their time fighting each other, but they'll figure it out soon enough. Word gets around fast. Players like to brag when they learn new information." I feel an urge, a yearning deep inside of me. I want to get out into the game world as soon as possible. "We should upgrade what we can and get moving."

"Sorry. It's getting late," Xen says, opening screens around his avatar. "I need to log out and get some sleep. Omniversalism teaches us that a good night's sleep keeps our wisdom close."

"Seriously? But we just started playing…"

Xen looks defeated and says with an annoyed tone, "We've been playing for hours. You can keep playing if you want, but I need to say goodnight to Raev and go to bed."

He's probably right. Time doesn't pass at the same speed inside the game as it does outside. If you play long enough, it can really mess with you. I still groan with disappointment.

"I'll see you tomorrow night," Xen says, ignoring my reaction. "Don't stay up too late. I want you full of energy for the concert."

I can see how happy the idea of me going to the concert makes him. His eyes are full of hope, even for something so silly. Why would my existence at this event be so important to him?

"Okay," I say, turning away and looking through the menu system, "whatever."

There's an awkward pause that I barely notice before I hear the announcer say, "Group member Xen has left the game."

I look over my shoulder and glance at the space he was just occupying. There's an emptiness that I don't recognize. Although the lack of his existence is more apparent than usual, I push the feeling away easily and return to the menu.

The amount of upgrades available to me is amazing. Everything from telescopic sights and attachable grenade launchers, to night-vision goggles and camouflage cloaks. I spend almost two hours scrolling through all the options, looking ahead at the items available to me that I can't yet afford. I choose what my meager sum of Koins will allow and select the "Complete Order" option. A damage-enhancing upgrade connects to the barrel on both of my pistols. An armored trench coat appears on my body, but without the dust-covered details I added to my original. It isn't much, but I already feel more powerful.

My stomach growls in the real world, and I feel it twist. I should log out, just for a moment, so that I can squirt some vitapaste into my mouth and get back into the game without the distraction, but the idea of trying out my new gear is too exciting.

Maybe just one more quest.

I open the menu screen and hundreds of different quests pour into my view. Glowing dots blink next to each listing, but they're all different colors. I look at the top of the screen and see a description explaining that white dots signify quests for my level range. I scroll around, searching for the quest that's closest to the equipment shop. I find one that's only a few blocks away, and select it. The brittle parchment rolls out of the screen, and the invisible pen starts writing the quest description for me to read.

"A UFO has crash landed in DangerWar City, infesting an entire park with bloodthirsty aliens. Eradicate the menace! You will be rewarded 3,000 Koins for your efforts."

Simple and straight forward. It makes sense for a low level quest. It was designed for a level 4 player, but I'm not worried. I open the sealed metal door and step back onto the city street, ready to get back in the game.

The street outside is silent in the darkness of the night. I can hear traffic and horns honking a few blocks away, but there aren't any NPC civilians wandering around on this side street. I look over at the military-style jeep crashed into the streetlight and jog toward it.

Without another group member, the mounted machine gun on the back is useless, but I'd rather be traveling with the speed of a vehicle than crossing the downtown area on foot. If the other players are still obsessed with killing each other, I need to stay out of their crossfire as much as possible.

I hope the streetlight didn't damage more than the front bumper. When I climb into the driver's seat and turn the key, the engine starts with no problem. I put the jeep in reverse and pull away from the lamppost. The metal scrapes loudly as the bumper unlocks from the pole. Without the jeep to brace it, the entire lamp topples over, smashing the glass cover around the bulb when it hits the pavement.

I turn on the headlights and stomp on the gas. The jeep rolls between the abandoned buildings around me, the sound of the engine bouncing off the brick walls. I blow past a stop sign and turn right onto a more well-used street. I see civilians and hear gunfire come from an alleyway as I slow down to fit between a taxi and a city bus. I step on the gas and pull away, putting the nearly pointless PvP violence behind me.

It only takes me a few minutes to reach the fenced-in park. It's tempting to burst through the gate with my new jeep, guns blazing, but that's impulsive and stupid. I park the jeep on the side of a business called a "pizza parlor" and creep across the street. With a running jump, I scramble up the fifteen-foot brick wall surrounding the park and peek over the top.

I see groups of alien beasts roaming under lamps sporadically set around the paved walkways, and in the center of the park is a smoldering spaceship. The aliens are humanoid looking, albeit with six glowing eyes and pale green skin. Every few moments, one of the beasts stops and howls into the air, exposing the rows of razor sharp teeth it hides inside its mouth. I try to count how many of the NPC enemies I'll need to kill, but I lose track around thirty or forty. I suck in a deep breath and swing my legs over the top of the fence. I drop down near a tree, peering out from behind the trunk. I'm not sure what's going to happen when I fire my first shot, but I'm hoping I can take on one enemy at a time.

I slide my guns from their holsters and take aim at the closest alien. With a single squeeze of the trigger, a bullet slams into the back of the alien's head, launching him forward, forcing its face into the ground. I don't wait to see if it's dead before I take aim on the next one. As I'm pulling the trigger, I hear the same howl that these creatures have been emitting, but this time it's deafening. The sound is coming from every single alien in the park, and when it stops, they all turn toward me.

When the creatures charge, I lose my breath for a second and unconsciously back step as I squeeze both triggers, slicing through the alien flesh and cutting them down one at a time. The violent animation is impressive every time a bullet strikes one, but when their bodies hit the ground, they explode into pixels, just like the players.

I swing the barrels to the left, using a wall of bullets to stop the creatures charging me from that direction. I don't kill every one that I strike, but I do enough damage to knock them down and stop them from advancing. I'm watching the line, the distance between their gaping maws and my avatar is getting smaller. I keep firing, blasting alien after alien, but the swarm doesn't stop. As I cut down a row of six or seven with one swooping motion of gunfire, I catch a glimpse of the crashed UFO, and I see more of the creatures pouring out from the back of the ship. They're replacing their fallen brethren as quickly as I can kill them, and the wall of snapping teeth is getting closer.

00001101

It's a losing battle, but I keep firing, hoping the game will at least award me Koins for how many of the beasts I can take down before I die.

I'm spending too much time focusing on the creatures coming from the left, and I don't see one of the aliens leap over a pile of corpses on my right. With two huge bounds, it stretches its arms and legs as far as it can and takes a final pounce toward me. It's too late. I can see its mouth opening, its teeth glittering in the lights, its tongue slathering spit from side-to-side, salivating at the thought of my blood. I have to admit, whoever designed these things did a pretty amazing job.

Before my brain can even register what's happening, the alien's head separates from its body, both of which fall to the ground, hard. My trigger finger stalls for a second as I watch it collapse into pixels. My brain is trying to catch up, but my body feels frozen in place.

"Keep firin', Cowboy!"

I hear the voice from behind me. It's a girl's voice, but it sounds husky and aggressive, twinged with that slang Mandarin accent that all the "cool kids" are using.

I see another group of aliens getting close to me, and the sight summons my brain back to the present. My finger twitches, and the bullets from my guns pound into the aliens again. I want to look behind me, but there's too many creatures. I can't take my eyes off them. I can't stop judging their distance and using instant calculations as to which enemy to fire at with the next bullet.

The girl behind me steps up to protect my flank from another group of aliens that are trying to sneak around a small rock formation. She's wearing a white kimono covered in yellow flowers, the silky material hanging heavier on her body than normal cloth. Maybe it has armor? White paint covers her emotionless face, and she's pulled her white hair up tight into two separate pigtails, tied with yellow ribbons. She's holding a wide-bladed sword that looks like it's twice her size, nearly a foot wide, and would require two hands to wield, but she's twirling it around in one hand like it weighs nothing.

She notices my distraction and says, "Stay focused, yo."

I keep firing, but my mind splits between my shooting strategy and the arrival of this new player. Is she trying to work with me, or is she trying to steal my quest? I consider blasting her when she turns her back, but I know that without her, I'm dead anyway.

When the group of aliens moves around the rock formation, the sword-wielding girl steps into position. Her movements are too fast to be real. Her body shudders and she flashes across a twenty-yard distance like an instant strike of lightning. She rotates her sword in an arc that splatters the entire group in a spinning blender of gore. Then she's back at my side in another flash.

"We're needin' to destroy that spaceship. It just keeps creatin' more," she yells over the flare of my gun.

"I noticed," I say. "How do you suggest we do that?"

She squints her eyes, looking past the mob of creatures I'm cutting down with my gunfire. There's a wall of injured bodies that the aliens are climbing over to get to us. It's slowing them down, but it's making it harder to judge their momentum, too.

"You seein' that engine?" she yells, pointing at the ship. "It's glowin' like the crash ruptured it. The fuel's lookin' volatile, yo."

Her slang accent sounds young and makes me want to write her off, but I take a quick glance and see that her assessment of the situation is accurate.

"I can't risk ignitin' it with my sword. I'd be too close to the explosion. I'll make an openin'. You're takin' the shot, Cowboy."

She doesn't even wait for me to agree to the strategy. She zips into the fray, swinging her sword to each side of her, slicing a path through the mob of beasts. In only a few seconds, there's a clear path straight toward the ship. I ignore the instinct to keep firing at the aliens that are near me and turn my guns. I focus both barrels on the glowing, toxic fuel that's pouring onto the ground. I pull both triggers at the same time. The fuel ignites.

The sword-wielding girl is already dashing away when the ship explodes, but we're both thrown to the ground from the concussive blast that emanates out from the ship in a glowing ring of energy. The sound makes my ears whine, and the flash blinds my eyes for a moment. When I catch my breath, and my eyes finally focus, I hear the announcer's voice.

"Quest completed. You have earned 3,000 Koins."

I rub my eyes, trying to help them focus. When I open them again, the girl dressed in a kimono is looking down at me.

"You're welcome, yo," she says sarcastically.

I'm waiting for her sword to impale me in a coup de grace, but instead she offers me her hand to help me to my feet. I accept it, and the familiar options of YES and NO pop up in front of me.

I hear the announcer ask, "Would you like to form a group?"

I hesitate longer than I did with Xen, and the girl is doing the same. We stand amongst the wreckage in the park, bodies burning all around us before disappearing into pixels, but we're just staring at each other. She's sizing me up, judging me with her eyes.

"I don't even know your name," I say.

She doesn't say anything for an uncomfortably long time. She finally sighs and says, "Fantom."

I tip my hat. "Arkade."

We both stand in silence, waiting for each other to make the decision on grouping. I still don't want her help, but I'm starting to realize I might need it. As long as it benefits me, maybe that outweighs the annoyance of interacting with another person.

I reach out and touch the YES that's floating in front of me. She slowly raises her hand and touches her own YES button. The glowing border surrounds her, and her location appears on my map.

"You figured out the questin'. Good for you," she says, sheathing her sword.

"It's worth more Koins," I say with a dull tone, stating a fact and nothing more.

We both turn when we hear gunfire nearby.

Fantom laughs. "Yeah, well, not everyone's figurin' that out so fast."

"They're still playing the old game, and until they learn the new rules, they'll just continue doing what they know."

Fantom shrugs her shoulders. "More Koins for us, yo."

"Exactly," I say with a smile. I point toward the pizza parlor. "I've got a vehicle. We should get moving to the next quest before any nosy players come to check out the explosion."

She gestures with her hand and says, "Lead the way, Cowboy."

We both hop the fence, and Fantom follows me to the jeep, jumping into the back and gripping both of her hands onto the mounted machine gun. "This could be fun, yo."

"Glad you like it." I climb into the driver's seat. "It'll be nice to have someone to fire that thing."

I zoom in on my map screen and check for the next closest quest. I find another one, but it's level 2. Now that I have a group, I'm willing to take on something a little harder.

"What level are you?"

"Level 7." She spins the gun around, testing its pivot speed. "You?"

All I say is, "Close to that." Then I direct the conversation back at her. "Why were you doing such a low level quest?"

She doesn't look at me, giving the question very little thought. "Maybe I wasn't doin' the quest, Cowboy. Maybe I was just helpin' you out."

"Doing your public service for the day?"

"Not so much. I guess I figured I'd be levelin' even faster if I had someone watchin' my back."

I frown, not completely believing her. "So... why me?"

"Why not? If you're figurin' out quests so quickly, then I'm guessin' you're at least a halfway decent player."

She says it with a sarcastic tone, but I think she means it playfully. I have a hard enough time reading people, and I'm starting to think she purposefully designed her painted face to not show any emotion.

"Seriously, Cowboy. I can tell you're good, yo. You must have played the original game."

I'm still trying to play it cool, so I start the engine of the jeep and shrug my shoulders. "Doesn't really matter if I did or not. This is a whole new game."

00001110

    We play for six straight hours. Fantom is such a skilled player that I find it surprising I've never seen her name on the old *DangerWar* scoreboard. She's quick-minded, making decisions on the fly that are always correct. If she moves right, death will be waiting for us on the left, and vice versa. I quickly learn that if she tells me to duck, I should kiss the floor. But she isn't trying to run the show, either. She has a great attitude about our group. She trusts my skills as a player, and as my levels grow over the next few hours, I start to trust myself. The game itself might be different, but the gameplay really isn't, and once I click into the mechanics, I'm an unstoppable death dealer once again.

    The only downside to Fantom is how chatty she can be. At first I think she's as focused on the game as I am, but over the course of the six hours, during our moments of downtime between quests, she keeps bringing up real world issues. When we're crawling through a sewer, hunting down the alligator-men who are threatening the city, she goes on and on about the global-political racism toward North Americans. I try to bring the subject matter back to the game by asking her to show me her inventory.

    "We need to understand each other's capabilities if we want to make sound decisions. Our strategy depends on it."

She agrees and we reveal our screens to each other. Her lightning fast movements are a result of a rare magical ring that the game rewarded her after she killed a quest boss early in the game. It feels unbalanced for a low level item, but as long as she's in my group, I'm not going to file a complaint. When I notice that her cloth kimono doesn't have armor like I thought, she has an annoyingly confident explanation.

"I ain't needin' armor cause I ain't plannin' on gettin' hit, yo."

Where I chose endurance and spent all my extra Koins bulking out my avatar with new protective gear, she chose dexterity. Luckily, the combination of our play styles merge well. I can take the hits in the center of the mayhem—just where I like to be—while she skirts the outside, picking off opponents with deadly accuracy.

After six hours of questing, I already gained seven more levels, making my avatar level 10. Fantom reaches level 12. The amount of Koins required to level-up increases exponentially every time you gain a new level, so it's an ever-increasing climb to the top, but it also means I'll eventually catch up to her, and we'll be moving at the same rate.

At nearly five in the morning, I'm leaping off a flagpole, firing at a swarm of gargoyles perched at the top of a courthouse. I barely hear the announcer in my ear over the crack of my pistols.

"Mandatory world-wide system reboot in thirty minutes."

The rare Anti-Gravity Belt the game awarded me for killing the Troll King at the end of the last quest lets me drop slowly to the ground so that I don't splatter against the street. I keep firing as I fall, chipping away at the last of the stone beasts. Finally they shatter, crumbling into pixels on the pavement below me.

Fantom comes bursting from a window, her sword impaled in the wizard we were hunting down because, according to the quest description, he had taken the mayor of DangerWar City hostage. She rips her sword from the wizard's chest and leaps off his falling corpse, launching herself toward my slow descent. I toss my gun into my other hand and reach out as far as I can. Our fingers touch, and I grasp tightly, catching her at the last second. I hear her let out a gasp as she swings below me, pulling my body faster toward the ground, but still at a safe descent. The landing is rough, but we wipe ourselves off and accept our Koins for completing yet another quest.

"Nice job," Fantom says, sliding her sword into the sheath on her back. "That was a close one, yo."

I raise my eyebrows. "You're telling me. What were you doing in there?"

"Exactly what I said I'd be doin'. Thanks for keepin' them minions off me."

I chuckle to myself and say, "I don't remember the plan including you leaping out of any windows just as I happen to be falling past."

She shrugs her shoulders and walks back toward the jeep, speaking over her shoulder. "That's what I call improvisin', yo."

We both sit in the front of the vehicle, relaxing as we gesture through our own screens, checking stats and quest locations. I see a nearby quest, but I'm not sure we'll have time to complete it. It would be useless to start if the system reboots before we can finish.

"Did you hear the announcement?"

Fantom nods. "Yeah. You disconnectin'?"

"Not a chance," I say. "It's Saturday. There's no school. I'm playing as much as I can this weekend."

She grins and looks at me out of the corner of her eye. "You still in DOTedu?"

I feel my face swell up, and I'm glad my avatar can't portray embarrassment. "Um. I mean… sort of."

She keeps grinning but turns her attention back to the screens in front of her. "You seem older than that. You ain't been actin' like no kid."

"I'm almost sixteen."

"Cool," she says, sounding as if she really doesn't care, either way.

"How old are you?" I ask, figuring with her pension for that slang accent that she must be young.

She makes a few more gestures and then takes one long swipe to close all the screens. She turns in her seat and looks at me. "Does it matter?"

I consider the question. "Actually, no."

"Yeah," she says. "I sorta figured, yo."

"What's that supposed to mean?"

She lets out an annoyed sigh and says, "It means I get the feelin' you ain't really carin' 'bout no real world. It's cool, yo. There're a lotta kids out there like you."

I roll my eyes. Now she sounds like an adult. The way she talks about the real world solidifies in my mind that she's one of "them." Someone like my father. Someone who still clings to the ideal that the real world has some greater value left to it. And to her, I'm on the other side, which is truer than she knows.

"Yeah," I say, speaking with a defiant tone. "You're right. I think anyone who'd choose the cold, empty existence of the real world over this," I wave my hands around, indicating the entire game world of *DangerWar*, "I think that person has something wrong with them. Or they're just stubborn."

"Not everyone's real world is cold and empty, yo. And the real world is, you know, *real*."

"And this isn't?"

"I'm wearin' a kimono with a sword strapped to my back, *and* I just killed a wizard."

"What's your point?"

She laughs.

I don't join in her laughter. "I'm serious."

She looks at me, surprised by my directness, then rubs her eyes and says, "This is all in your head. Your body ain't got nothin' to do with it."

"And why is my body important? Isn't my mind who I actually am? As long as my brain is present, then so am I."

"Whatever, yo," she says. "You're soundin' like that philosophy stuff I gotta study."

I grin knowingly. "So you're still in school, too?"

She scoffs. "Barely. I'm goin' to the University next year. I gotta do prep work."

I roll my eyes. "The university is still DOTedu."

"Yeah, but I'm gettin' real people teachin' me, not some NPCs."

"Real? But it's still an avatar. According to you, that's not real at all."

"You know what I mean, yo."

"Yeah, I do. But I'm not sure you know what you mean."

There's a pause as the thought sinks in, causing her to shake her head. "You're kinda frustratin', yo."

I shrug my shoulders, and a mocking grin creeps across my face.

The announcer breaks up the debate. "Mandatory world-wide system reboot in ten minutes."

Fantom stretches her arms. "I'm gonna scram. No point waitin' for the forced log-out."

"Okay," I say. "I'm going to try to do some shopping while I can. Will I see you after the reboot?"

She smiles and says, "Not sure, Cowboy. I guess you'll hafta wait and see. Might be somethin' better happenin' in the real world, you know?"

Before I can answer, her avatar lowers in resolution, turning into fewer and fewer pixels until it completely disappears.

"Group member Fantom has left the game."

I start up the engine of the jeep and pull out from the curb, weaving through traffic. I hear no gunfire and see no players. I feel like the last man alive. This is the dead time, the time of day when the fewest possible players are logged-in. It's why the system operators choose this time to reboot the world. It interrupts the experience for the fewest players.

I reach the equipment shop with only a minute to spare. I park the jeep next to the destroyed lamp post, but instead of going inside, I climb to the top of the equipment store and decide to watch the game world reboot from the rooftop. It's the gamer's version of watching the sunset.

A timer appears during the last sixty seconds, counting down until the reboot. Off in the distance, I see that same jet fighter that Xen wants to fly so badly skimming through the clouds. It makes me think of him. I'm dreading the concert. Not because I have to meet his girlfriend, or sit through some music I probably won't like, but because it will take me out of the game during a prime gaming hour. Who knows how many Koins Fantom will be able to rack up while I'm sitting in some DOTsoc club pretending to enjoy myself?

The countdown reaches the last few seconds, and I ready myself for the forced log-out. Then, just as the timer reaches the final second, I swear I hear screaming. Not the sound of one person screaming, or even a large group, but the sound of millions of people screaming all at once. It hits me with a crushing force, but before my ears can register the noise, *DangerWar 2* evaporates, shattering into a billion pixels like one giant avatar that just suffered a head shot.

00001111

My eyes flutter open, and I'm looking at the inside of my E-Womb. I try to sit up slowly, but the hunger in my stomach wrenches me forward, twisting itself into knots before pushing vomit up through my throat. I spit out clear streams of liquid.

The bottom of the sphere is full of a cold liquid. I urinated hours ago and never felt it inside NextWorld. The nanomachines don't block the feeling, so I must have been so enthralled with the action that I didn't even notice. I can't say it didn't cross my mind that it was far past the time to relieve myself, but I didn't want to care. I want one of those new E-Wombs so badly. Then I wouldn't *have* to care.

The real world is just so messy.

I force my arms to pull me from the sphere in the wall, and I hobble toward the mirrored screen. I insert my finger into the scanner. Seconds later the dispenser opens, and I snatch the tube of vitapaste from the opening. I unscrew the cap and squeeze an entire mouthful of the goo between my lips. My gums mash it around for a few seconds before I swallow. I almost choke on the amount I'm trying to force down my throat. As soon as it's down, I'm squeezing more into my body. I empty the tube in three large mouthfuls, then jam my finger back into the machine. I need to fill up on as much as I can stomach so that I can last in the game world for as long as possible.

The second tube goes down slower. I take the time in between squeezes to glance up at the screen above the sink. The message icon is flashing, with a number four next to it. Three messages from my father. One message from Fantom. I select Fantom's first.

A video-cast enlarges onto the screen. Her avatar is standing outside the gates of *DangerWar*. The crowd of people has mostly dispersed, with only a few fanatics still camping around the area. She waves at the virtual camera and smiles.

"I was just wantin' to say thanks for your help, yo. I didn't get a chance to do that before I logged-out. I was thinkin' we need to find someone else to join our group. The stronger we are, the higher level quests we'll be doin'. The more players that start questin', the harder it's gonna be to find lower level stuff. We need to start jumpin' ahead. Anyway, if you're on this afternoon, I'll find you. Get some sleep, yo."

The video-cast shrinks back into the envelope icon on the screen. The disappearance sends a sensation through me that I'm not comfortable with. It's so foreign to me that I don't recognize it. The attention is weird. Spending so much time with someone else is weird. All of it is... *weird*. I've spent hours upon hours inside *DangerWar*, but I restricted my socialization to killing other players. There was no talking or cooperation. There was no helping anyone or saving anyone, and I never received a "thank you" for any of my actions.

I consider reading my dad's messages, but I know what they'll say. More guilt trips and requests for real world meetings. I delete them without opening them.

I grab a towel from my closet and soak up all the moisture from the E-Womb. I toss the damp towel into the automated washer and sit down on my bed. I only mean to take a small rest, but before I know it, my eyelids are feeling heavy. My head droops, my neck unable to lift it any longer.

I jerk awake, but now I'm lying in bed. I can see artificial daylight drifting through the metal shutters on my window, and I wonder how long I've been asleep. I feel panic as I rub my eyes and try to focus on the screen above my sink. The clock in the corner reads 14:17, and my heart sinks. I've wasted too much time. Fantom could already be playing, filling her treasure chest full of Koins without me.

I rush to the E-Womb, but before I crawl in, I decide to be smart about it. I use the toilet and let the vitapaste dispenser scan my finger. I choke down three tubes of the goo as fast as I can. My heart is racing. I need to make up for lost time. With remnants of vitapaste still hanging from the corner of my mouth, I crawl through the doorway into the sphere of my E-Womb. The door seals shut, and the lights fill the interior. I rub my arms, letting them acclimate to the warmth again, and then I settle into a comfortable position.

"Log in."

My vision goes black, but soon enough I appear in front of the *DangerWar* gate. The crowds of people have gathered again, and I see a few players doing interviews with newscasters. If they aren't careful about what they say, they're going to find themselves with banned accounts. They're seeking fame when they should be playing. No one will care about them in a few months when the game goes public anyway. People will still care about me. My avatar will be at the top of the scoreboard, with a head start that no one will be able to match. Then I remember the level 72 player that killed me in my first few moments of playing.

Grael.

I shake the sinking feeling. I'll beat him. At that point in the game, the Koins you need to reach the next level must be astronomical. I'll catch up to him eventually. I just need to dedicate myself.

I check my inventory, see my *DangerWar 2* beta key still inside, and then step through the door. My avatar reappears right where the game kicked me out, looking out over the city from the rooftop of the equipment store. I climb back down to the street. I notice right away that my jeep is no longer there, which doesn't surprise me, but I also notice that the lamp post looks repaired, as if nothing ever touched it. The system reboot set everything back to the default settings. I check the quest log and see that everything we completed has reset as well. Every NPC that was killed is alive again.

I reenter the shop and open the holographic screen so that I can spend some of my loot. My Koins are spilling over from my treasure chest. I purchase a few armor upgrades, like always, but this time I purchase another damage upgrade for both of my guns. I also purchase a pair of telescopic goggles that hang around my neck, only because I figure they must be more useful than their bargain price would lead me to believe. Probably because everyone focuses on the weapons and armor, not the tools.

Once my Koin account is empty, I step out from the equipment shop and back into the game world. An alert pops up in front of me, letting me know that I'm receiving a direct audio-cast from a group member. I touch the icon, and I hear Fantom's voice in my ear.

"Glad you finally decided to show up, yo."

"I was… taking a nap."

"The real world finally come knockin'?"

"I guess."

"Don't sweat it, yo. We're all havin' to answer the door at some point."

"Unfortunately."

"The map's sayin' you're outside an equipment shop."

"The map never lies."

"Good. We're on our way."

"We? I was only gone for a few hours and you already replaced me?"

"Stop whinin', yo. We got a new group member."

I cringe. I don't really want to meet anyone new, let alone play with them, but I know that Fantom is right. We need to take on harder quests. And as much as I hate to admit it, I'm pretty sure I can trust her judgment. I mean, she chose to group with me, right?

I stand next to the doorway for almost five minutes, bored and considering messaging Fantom again to see what's taking them so long. As I'm opening an audio-cast screen to do so, I hear the sound of tires as they struggle to hold onto the corner. I look down the street and spot a blood red sports car rolling toward me. I step behind a parked car on the street and ready my guns, but as the car draws closer, I can see the highlighted outlines of group members sitting in the front seats. The car comes to a stop right in front of the equipment shop and both doors flip open.

I see Fantom get out of the driver's side and a very young boy step out of the passenger side. He's wearing very regular clothes for his age. A backwards baseball cap, baggy shorts, and a t-shirt with some kind of animated video-cast character on it. As I holster my guns and walk toward him, I can see his skin looks carved from wood, like his body is a marionette without any strings. I've seen similar fairy tale avatars in DOTkid. They were expensive gifts for spoiled children.

"Arkade," Fantom says, "meet Ekko."

The wooden boy runs up to me, holding out his hand for me to shake, but his avatar is shifting around, flickering back and forth. His entire image looks shaky and jittery. He blinks out of sight, then he's suddenly behind me.

"Sorry," he says bashfully. "I don't have the best connection. My tower is in Old Mongolia."

"He's got lag, yo," Fantom says offhandedly, "but we're needin' another player, and he's the same level as us."

"Lag? He's barely staying connected." I'm looking at him like he smells funny. "My friend Xen could catch up to us in a few hours. We don't need some little kid tagging along for the ride."

"Hey," the kid says, about to poke his hand into my chest, but his avatar shudders and he's suddenly standing two feet to the left. He re-calibrates his view and says, "I'm not a little kid."

His voice is high-pitched, but his accent is the exact opposite of Fantom. It's dripping with the old Mandarin emphasis on words.

His image shakes again. As it jitters back and forth, I slice my hand straight through his chest.

"Look at this. It's ridiculous. I'm not putting my life in the hands of some kid who breaks in and out of the game at random."

"We've been doin' fine, yo," Fantom says. "We've been questin' for hours."

"The lag really doesn't bother me," Ekko says with a chipper attitude. "I barely notice."

"Good for you," I say, walking away from him, "but *I* notice. Sorry kid, but maybe Old Mongolia just isn't meant to play games."

Fantom shrugs her shoulders, spits on the ground, and says, "Fine. We ain't needin' you, so you ain't comin' with us." Then she looks at Ekko and says, "Let's get movin', yo. We're gonna be needin' to find more group members before we go takin' on the Titans." She flashes a grin back at me. "And we're gonna be needin' to buy some upgrades with all them Koins we been makin'." She walks back toward the sports car.

The kid looks back at me with a panicked look on his face and then chases after her. "Fantom, wait. Hold on."

"What?" she snaps, as she opens the driver side door.

"Listen," the boy says in a hushed tone, but I can still hear him. He's glancing over at me from the corner of his eyes as he says, "You said he was one of the best players you've seen so far."

"I was exaggeratin'," she says, looking right at me. "There're other players, and they're probably better. This cowboy ain't nothin' special, yo. Besides, I ain't lettin' nobody act like that toward someone just because of where they're from."

"Great," I yell out, my anger cutting through my teeth. "Good luck finding someone else! You know, I thought you were smart, but you're choosing this kid over me? I guess I overestimated you, Fantom."

She doesn't respond. She doesn't even look at me. She slams her car door shut, stepping on the gas pedal to express herself with the sounds of the engine. Ekko begs me with his eyes, but when I don't respond, he drags his wooden feet, making his way around the car toward the passenger side. Fantom hesitates with a few more pushes of the gas pedal. I think she's waiting to see if I change my mind. I cross my arms, unmoving.

The tires spin on the pavement, and the car launches right at me. I have to jump to the side so that she doesn't hit me, and I watch the car disappear down the street. The announcer's voice ricochets in my ear.

"Fantom and Ekko have left the group."

/eye/zero

00010000

Now I remember what I hate about playing with other people. There's always some emotions that get in the way, or some labyrinthine social structure that I don't understand. I always end up offending someone or saying the wrong thing, and then I have to waste all my time apologizing and trying to make them feel better instead of playing the game.

I'm not sad that Fantom left. I'm not even angry. All I have to do is remind myself that this means I can keep all the Koins for myself. No more sharing. And then all I have to do is ignore the fact that I'm back to playing low level quests.

I spend the next five hours grinding through the easy stuff, taking the few Koins the game awards me, and moving on to the next quest. My treasure chest slowly fills, but not quickly enough. I start taking risks in the fourth hour, completing quests that are a level or two higher than me. I'm careful, patient, and methodical. Even so, I manage to get myself killed a couple of times, thrown back outside the *DangerWar* gates, but I only lose a small amount of Koins as a penalty. In the end, my skills win out, and I start jumping levels at a faster rate. By the eighth hour, I'm level 20, and I'm not missing Fantom or that kid. I remember how sharp I become when I'm alone with nothing to distract me. There's no such thing as greed or selfishness when I only need to worry about myself.

At the top of my ninth hour inside of *DangerWar 2*, I'm fighting a werewolf motorcycle gang. I'm standing in the center of a parking lot, and the pack is swarming around me, their bikes roaring with a kind of throaty burp as they circle me. They all look quite bulky, with hair sprouting from underneath their leather jackets. The bikers lash out with whip-like chains attached to their belts. At the end of the chain hangs a softball-sized metal sphere covered in hooks and spikes. The chain is short, but it magically gains links when thrown, extending toward me, then retracting back. Lucky for me, none of them have struck me. Yet.

I keep dodging and firing, stepping left and right, ducking the crude weapons. I'm trying to read their pattern of attack. It feels random at first, but I know there's no such thing as random in programming. The pattern might be lengthy, and it's possible that it's too long for me to remember, but I doubt it. The main problem is, every time I think I might be getting close to understanding it, I manage a lucky shot and kill one of the bikers as they drive past me, and that changes the pattern.

I give up on my strategy and make a run for the hole that the biker I just dropped left in the circle. I scoop up his handlebars and upright the bike as the gang swoops around for another pass. I duck a chain and jump down onto the kick start lever. The cycle roars to life perfectly, and I pull back on the throttle as another spiked ball comes flying through the air. This one barely misses the back of my head as my acceleration pulls me away.

I bring the combat out onto the road, and the bikers follow me. I've shot enough of them to make them determined to kill me, and no amount of fleeing is going to deter them, which is exactly what I was counting on. They keep up with me, actually gaining on me once we hit a straightaway. This is what the designers created them for, so their driving skills don't surprise me. My advantage comes from the fact that at these speeds, they can't keep throwing their chains at me. They try, but not only does the momentum work against them, their aim is worse while they're dodging between the other vehicles on the road.

I keep my right hand on the throttle, and with my left hand I slide one of my pistols out of its holster. I set the gun in my lap and watch the gang in my rear-view mirror. I try to gauge their formation and speed. When their bikes separate enough from each other, I clench both hands, squeezing the brakes and melting my tires into the street. The bikers go flying past, unready for the sudden stop. As soon as they do, I pull back on the throttle again and launch after them.

I grab the pistol from my lap and fire, sinking three bullets into the back of a wolf-man's leather jacket. He goes spinning out of control and smashes into oncoming traffic. The other three slow down, swinging their chains now that they have an advantageous momentum. They toss the spiked balls at me, but I swerve the bike back and forth, letting the chains slide past my head, only missing me by inches. I pull the trigger on my gun again and manage a head shot. The werewolf slumps forward on his bike. It veers right and plows into a building.

The other two bikers grow annoyed with my placement and slow their bikes down even more, trying to get next to me. We all keep swerving in between traffic, still moving faster than the speed limit. Two city dump trucks, driving side-by-side, force the bikers apart. I slide between the two huge vehicles and yank out my other pistol, holding both weapons out to the sides. As I come out from between the trucks, the bikers try to converge on me, but as soon as they see the guns pointed at them, the shock on their hairy faces is unmistakable. I pull both triggers and knock the bikers from their cycles. The dump trucks bounce a little as they run over the bodies.

I slide both guns into my holsters and grab onto the handlebars as the announcer awards me my Koins. Then I turn onto a side street and point my cycle back toward the equipment shop. The streets are full of players. It's the prime time for gaming, and everyone who has a beta key is playing. Thankfully, the players have figured out that quest combat is the way to go in this game, so no one acts aggressive toward me in the slightest. I roll through the streets, watching players running down sidewalks carrying all kinds of different weapons or driving past me in all kinds of different vehicles, all on their way to different quests. The virtual wind is blowing in my face, cool and refreshing.

I'm exactly where I want to be.

I arrive at the equipment shop a little before midnight, and when I get inside, I kick back in front of the holographic screen, taking my time as I peruse each menu. I have enough Koins to splurge, so I really enjoy myself. The silence inside the equipment shop is a welcome contrast to the gunfire I've been listening to all night. I let myself relax, swiping through screens for almost two hours. When I finally select "Confirm Purchase," I hear the announcer's voice in my ear.

"Group member Xen has entered the game."

I feel my heart sink into my stomach. Nothing pushes the breath in my lungs out. It simply evaporates. I can't turn around, even though I know his monk avatar just spawned behind me.

"I *knew* it," he says. "I knew you were still in here. You're actually that big of a—"

I spin around and cut off his accusations. "Oh man. Oh wow. I'm *really* sorry, Xen. I totally forgot. I got caught up in questing, and I lost track of—"

This time, he cuts me off, holding up his hand and turning his head away as if he can't face my excuses. "Don't bother. I should have known better."

"It's not like that."

"It's *exactly* like that."

"Xen. I'm sorry."

"Do you know how long Raev and I waited for you outside the venue? We missed the first three songs because I kept telling her not to worry. I kept telling her you'd be there. Because you promised."

I rub my forehead, feeling a headache coming on already. I hate stress, and I hate confrontation even more. Social confrontation anyway. If we could settle this with battleaxes, I'd be much happier.

"I'll make it up to you. And Raev. When is the next concert?"

"I don't want you to come to the next concert."

I cringe, but manage to weakly ask, "Why not?"

"I don't want you there, Kade. Because you embarrassed me tonight. You made me look like a fool in front of the girl I love. I sat there and felt the need to explain to her why I'm your friend. I had to make excuses for you. I never want to do that again. Omniversalism teaches us to always forgive, but to never forget."

I mumble, "I'm sorry," again and look at the floor, wishing I knew how to make everything better.

"Stop saying that."

"I don't know what else to say."

"But I know you don't mean it."

"I do."

"No, you don't. Do you really wish you had spent time at the concert with me instead of leveling your character? Do you actually regret all the fun you had tonight?"

I'm silent. I'm pondering his question and trying to force myself to lie, but he sees it in my eyes. My incredibly well-designed, highly-detailed eyes.

"That's what I figured."

"It's not like that, Xen. This is… this game world is my life. It's all I have."

"This game is all you *want*. And if this is all you want, then pretty soon this will be all you have."

Now he's making me angry. Now he's trying to hurt me as much as I hurt him. I speak without thinking.

"Maybe this game is all I *need*."

As soon as I say it, I feel the burn on my tongue. My words are like a flaming sword, and I just stabbed my best friend with them.

"I'm truly sorry you feel that way, Kade. I wish you could find a balance, like me. But I can see now that you don't really need me. Not in this game, and not in your life."

He gestures in the air, and I know he's opening his log-out screen. I open my mouth to say something, to make him stay, but my brain can't come up with anything. I see him glance at me one last time, then select the log-out button.

But nothing happens.

00010001

I don't hear the announcer tell me that Xen has left the game, nor does his avatar disappear. I see him frown in frustration, and he pushes the log-out button. Again. But nothing happens. Again.

"Why can't I log out?"

"Are you selecting the right option?" I ask, unable to see his screen.

"Of course I am."

"Are you sure?"

"There's one giant button that says 'log out,' so I'm guessing that's the button I'm supposed to push."

"Close all the screens and try it again."

He lets out a strained sigh and swipes the screens shut with his hand. With another few swipes, he reopens them and gestures through the menus. I see him reach out and touch the button again with the same result.

"Kade. What's going on?"

"I don't know."

He keeps jamming on the button.

"What's it doing?" I ask. "Is it registering your selection at all?"

"Yes," he says and I can hear a twinge of panic in his voice. "The button sinks in like I selected it, but…"

He punches the button with his fist, over and over. "Hey!" he yells. "Let me out of this stupid game!"

"Settle down."

"No!" The word shatters against my ears. "I won't settle down. I want to get out of here. I want to go spend time with someone who actually appreciates me. I don't even want to look at you, Kade."

I try to keep my voice calm as I say, "Okay. Fine. Just let me help you. Back out of that menu and open the instant messenger. You can talk to one of the system operators. They should be able to help you."

He growls in response and swipes in the air, doing what I said. He opens an audio-cast and records a message.

"My avatar name is Xen, and I can't log out of your stupid game. Get me out of here as soon as possible. I don't care how. Reboot me, delete me, whatever. I won't be playing anymore." He selects the send button and crosses his arms. A few seconds later he throws his hands into the air and screams. "Message cannot be sent!"

"What the heck is going on?"

"You tell me!"

I open my own menu, and the log out button appears in front of me. I gently push it in. It sinks into the air, lighting up to signify my choice, but nothing happens. When I let go, the button returns to its previous position.

"Xen, something is messed up with the game."

"I can see that."

"It's not working for me either."

"So we're trapped in here?"

I don't know how to reply other than to shrug my shoulders to hide my own increasing amount of dread. "I'm sure it will be fine. They're probably trying to fix the problem right now, and players are flooding them with messages, which is why they shut down their mailbox."

"Now what? I have to sit here and wait?"

"I'm sure we'll get an announcement soon. We just need to be patient."

Xen sits down on the floor and leans up against the wall behind him. "I guess I should have expected something like this." He laughs to himself in a way that lets me know he's the only one who finds it amusing. "It's a perfect ending to this night, in an ironically painful kind of way."

I'm trying to think of something witty to say, some sort of comeback that will turn this all around, but if I'm being honest, all I can think about is trying out the new explosive rounds I purchased.

Xen catches me glancing at the door, and he laughs, darkly. "Please don't tell me that you're thinking about playing right now?"

"No," I say, too quickly to be honest. "I mean, that's not—"

"I'm stuck here in your stupid game, and all you can think about is getting back out there and earning more Koins?"

I shrug my shoulders, and with very little enthusiasm I say, "I mean… if we're stuck here, there's no reason to just sit here and waste our time."

Xen's face shows no emotion. He's studying me like I'm some sort of science experiment gone terribly wrong. "Is that what this is to you?"

"What are you talking about?"

"This. Right here. Right now. Talking to me is a waste of time?"

I roll my eyes. "We're not talking, Xen. *You're* talking. You're telling me how horrible of a friend I am. Repeatedly. You're saying it in different ways, but you're saying the same thing. I get it. I suck." My words are energetic now. I'm able to turn this around on him, though I know I'm in the wrong. I feel worse about this action, but my mouth keeps moving. "So yes, Xen. If you really want to know the truth, I'd absolutely enjoy being out there, having fun and killing monsters, rather than sitting in here and listening to you tell me how badly I screwed up tonight."

"You know very well that this is about more than just tonight."

I scream through my teeth. "Fine! Whatever! Sit in here and do nothing. I don't care. But I'm going out there, and I'm going to have fun."

I start toward the door, but Xen stands up and says, "Wait."

I stop, but I don't turn around, and I don't look at him.

"Look," he says, "I know I'm letting my emotions get the best of me. This is—the way I'm reacting right now—this isn't how my religion teaches me to react. Omniversalism is about acceptance of everyone, no matter how they choose to live their life. It's about the balance between right and wrong, and being the counterweight when one outweighs the other."

I rub my forehead and groan. "Do you actually think you make sense when you talk like that?"

He smiles calmly and says, "What I'm trying to say is that Omniversalism teaches me that if I think you're being a bad friend, then I need to be a better friend. This will balance the flow. If your grip is loose, I must squeeze even tighter."

"And I suppose that was meant to be the simplified version?"

"Just accept my apology, Kade."

There's guilt in my stomach. He's taking the higher road, and I'm not even on the map. I feel bad for what I've done, but I'll feel bad if I accept his apology, and I'll feel bad if I don't. Maybe this is his point. Maybe this is part of his plan. Or maybe he's not as conniving as I am. Maybe he really is as naïve as he wants to be.

"You don't need to apologize, Xen."

"And I'm telling you, Kade, that neither do you. Let's move beyond this."

I nod and turn around, meeting his gaze. He's smiling, and I can't help mirroring his image. I don't want to accept his friendship. I think I'm better off without it. I'm safer. It's easier. I don't want to worry about anyone other than myself. It's too complex. But Xen is persistent.

"Thank you, Xen," I say through my smile.

He steps toward me and opens his thin arms. He wraps his skeletal biceps around me and squeezes. I find no comfort in the expression, only awkwardness. I feel confined. I feel misplaced.

"Okay, okay," I say from strained lungs. "You better stop before this hug becomes PvP."

He laughs a hearty laugh, a laugh like the Xen I've always known. He lets go and slaps both my shoulders. "You're right, my friend. If we're stuck here for a while, I might as well try to enjoy myself. Omniversalism teaches us that we should take advantage of all that life has to offer us. Pleasure isn't evil, and we shouldn't feel guilty about partaking in it."

"You don't have to join me."

"We make a good team, do we not?"

I want to point out the fact that we only played together for a minimal amount of time. I want to point out the fact that he's level 3 and I'm level 20, so either we play quests that are worth nothing to me, or I spend all my time keeping him alive.

I do neither.

"Yeah, Xen. We make a good team."

He summons a ball of green fire in his hand and says, "Then what are we waiting for?"

I turn back toward the entrance. When the armored door slides up to reveal the outside street, the sound is what overtakes me first. The echoes of gunfire pour inside the equipment shop. Explosions erupt from down the street. The screams of the dying barely break through the pounding noises of weaponry and magic. I'm staring in awe at the chaos that confronts me. My brain is unable to catch up to the action, and I'm afraid that my frozen stance is simply waiting to die. The flares from muzzles are constant, but between the nearly hypnotic strobe effect, I see the red sports car that Fantom and Ekko drove off in earlier that afternoon—now filled with bullet holes and smoke pouring out of the hood—come to a screeching halt right in front of my door. I see one figure firing from the window of the vehicle, but through the haze of smoke and debris, I can't tell who it is. Gunfire is chasing them from down the street, and it never stops.

The driver looks in my direction, and when our eyes lock, I recognize her as Fantom. She screams something to the figures in the car. The short wooden boy named Ekko that I met earlier opens the passenger side door and fires toward the hail of bullets coming at them. A female player steps out of the back seat, dragging something behind her, but I still can't see any details in the smoldering darkness.

"What's going on?" Xen yells over the cracking sounds of war.

"I don't know," is all I manage to say.

"Do you know those people?"

I pause for a second, trying to put an explanation into my mouth, but all I come up with is, "Yes."

Xen doesn't hesitate, stepping past me and saying, "We've got to help them."

"Wait!" I yell, expecting the crossfire to chew his low level avatar to pieces, but somehow he manages to hurl his spells at the unseen attackers without them mowing him down instantly.

I'm hesitating for far too long, and it's only when a bullet strikes Xen's leg and drops him to one knee that I finally leap out from the safety of my doorway. I glance both ways and see the pulsating flares of gunfire with the occasional brightness of a magical spell, but through the cloud of smoke, I can't see who's attacking. It feels like an army. A very big army. I fire both pistols, targeting the muzzle flashes, hoping to hit whatever is holding the weapons creating them.

The wooden boy runs up next to me, his image still shifting and flickering randomly. He's firing the opposite direction with an assault rifle upgraded with an unrealistic amount of additions, making it look like it should be impossible to lift, much less shoot. Fantom makes her way to the doorway, but never leaves the side of the other female player, who's still dragging something large across the street. Fantom is blocking the incoming fire with a glowing shield on her arm—obviously an upgrade she acquired during her higher levels, and one that negates her motto of, "I ain't needin' armor cause I ain't plannin' on gettin' hit, yo."

As I'm watching her, a bullet slams into my chest. My armor absorbs the damage, but it knocks me back a few steps. I keep firing.

"Everyone inside!" Fantom yells, grabbing me by the collar of my trench coat and yanking me through the doorway.

Ekko is next through the door, his wooden body gasping for air, as if he was only now able to breathe.

From down the street I hear someone yell, "Don't let them get inside the equipment shop!" and a horrendous sound of growls, screeches, and unearthly gurgling noises follow it in a chant of acknowledgment.

Xen steps back through the doorway, still tossing green fireballs until the last possible second, his face showing neither anxiety nor fear. The female player is the last through the door, wrapped in hundreds of leather straps and buckles, she's dragging the body of yet another player. She gives the body one final yank through the doorway, then topples over onto her back. Her hair is a bright yellow, and shaved close to her head, spiky and rough. Her lipstick matches the color of her black leather straps. As easy as it is to see every curve in her outfit, I can't help thinking how sharp her features make her appear. Like the blade of a knife.

She looks up at me, and I catch myself pausing to admire her. If she designed her avatar herself, she spent an incredible amount of time sculpting her face. There's a perfection to it that comes from the obvious idiosyncratic imperfections. It's the uniqueness of every detail, every line, every mark, that makes it so consuming. It's a brief respite from the chaos entering the equipment shop. She's a warrior of beauty amongst the ugliness of war.

00010010

"My... my name is Xen," the frail monk says. He sets his hand on Fantom's shoulder and asks, "Are you okay?"

She doesn't look at him, replying with only a slow nod of her head.

I step toward the player that the leather-strapped woman dragged into the room, but when I do, I immediately step back at the sight of him. Half of his head is missing, and I can see the pixelated insides, drifting around like broken code.

"What *is* that?" I ask, taking another step away.

"That's Klok," Fantom says. "He... he's part of our group."

"What's wrong with him? What's wrong with his avatar?"

"We don't know," Ekko says. "He tried to force a log out."

I start to ask, "What do you—" but I realize halfway through the sentence what they mean.

Fantom speaks bluntly, without any kind of remorse or hesitancy. "He shot himself, yo. But he ain't disappearin' like he's supposed to."

"What was going on out there?" Xen asks. "It looked like a war. More than usual, I mean."

"And who's this?" I ask, pointing at the player in leather straps and buckles, my words sounding more aggressive than I mean them.

"I'm Cyren." Her voice sounds faint, like she barely has the strength left to speak.

"I'm Arkade."

She smiles for the first time, and I lose myself in her for a second, but Ekko starts talking, and he breaks me from the magnetism.

"It *is* a war out there. As soon as word got out that the log-out function wasn't working… everyone started freaking out."

"But it ain't the players attackin' us," Fantom says. "It was the NPCs, yo."

I'm sure my confusion shows on my face.

"But the NPCs always attack, right?" Xen asks. "I thought that was part of the game."

I find his inexperience embarrassing. "Not out in the streets. Not unless you're in a quest. There should only be those civilian NPCs."

Fantom shakes her head and says, "The civilians are gone, yo. The streets looked empty at first, which is creepy enough, but then the NPCs from the quests started wanderin' around. Monsters, and wizards, and every demented thing in this game. They're wanderin' the streets, killin' players without any rhyme or reason."

"The game is…" Ekko starts, before rubbing his face and saying, "*broken.*"

"You're sure this isn't just part of the game?" Xen asks, looking at all of us, any of us, for confirmation.

"Maybe," Ekko says. "I mean, I guess that could be part of the game. But they'd never lock people in. It all feels connected."

I let everything they're saying sink in for a moment, but my mouth speaks before I'm ready. I glance at Fantom and say, "I'm surprised you decided to come here."

She scowls at me. "Trust me, it wasn't my first choice, yo."

"We made our way to the rooftops," Ekko says, interjecting into our little staring contest, "which worked for a while. We were able to hold off the ones on foot. But then the flying NPCs spotted us."

Fantom looks troubled by the memory as she mumbles, "There were hordes of winged demons. Like black clouds swoopin' down from the sky, yo."

"We weren't really sure what to do," Ekko says. "We saw players dying left and right, and none of them were disappearing. It was... it was kind of horrible to watch."

"Why aren't the players disappearing?" Xen asks. "What's happening to them?"

We're all silent for a moment, pondering the question, until Cyren offers an answer. "If you don't log-out, but your avatar is dead, you'd get stuck in the code."

"What does that mean in the real world?"

I say what we're all thinking. "It wouldn't be any different from a coma. A sleep that you couldn't wake up from."

"They'd have to unplug you just to wake you up," Ekko adds. "And we've all seen what happens when they do a cold shutdown of the E-Womb. The shock would corrupt your nanomachines. I don't think you want to risk the effect that would have on your body."

There's a pause as we all try to shake off the creeping terror that thought brings.

It's Xen who finally speaks, trying to push us out of the darkness. "Omniversalism teaches us that the unknown is what we fear the most. We shouldn't dwell on what *might* happen. We need to focus on what *did* happen and, more importantly, what *is* happening."

Ekko nods. "Agreed."

Xen smiles and says, "So tell us what you did next. When you were no longer safe on the rooftops, you decided to come here?"

"We weren't sure what to do," Ekko says, his wooden avatar blinking out of existence, then reappearing just as fast.

Fantom's face darkens as she humbles herself enough to say, "You gotta understand, everythin' was after us. *Everythin'*, yo."

Ekko says, "Klok was the one who checked the map to see where we should run."

"That's when all the quests were disappearin'," Fantom says. "Cyren's the one who thought of the equipment shop."

Ekko flickers as he says, "It made sense. It was the only place we were going to be safe."

I nod at Cyren and say, "That was smart."

She shrugs her shoulders and gives me the briefest of smiles.

"But Klok's an idiot," Fantom says. "He wouldn't listen to her. To any of us. He got the idea in his head that this was the game's way of loggin' everyone out. He didn't care what the graphics were showin'. He thought if we died, we'd be respawnin' outside the *DangerWar* gates. Back in NextWorld."

"How do we know he's wrong?" Xen asks.

I audibly scoff at him and point at the disturbing avatar on the floor. "Do you really want to take that risk?"

"This was the closest shop," Cyren says. "But we still had to get across nearly twenty blocks full of NPCs."

"You made it across twenty blocks?"

"Most of the stuff out there's from low level zones," Fantom says. "But the sheer number of them…"

I let my mouth speak before my brain filters my words again. "Were the NPCs still worth Koins?"

Fantom lets out a heavy sigh, and I can feel Xen's judgmental stare without looking at him.

"If they ain't stayin' in their quest zones, even level 30 players like us ain't gonna be able to hold out forever, yo. Can you imagine what would happen if the NPCs from the high level zones are wanderin' into the city? We all saw that dragon up in the mountain zone, right?"

I cringe when she drops that little tidbit of knowledge about being level 30. They've been busy. And they've been completing higher Level quests than me. Much higher. My own level 20 avatar suddenly feels incredibly weak.

I open screens in front of me to check the news-casts, or video-casts, or even the audio-casts, but nothing is connecting.

"Don't even bother tryin'," Fantom says. "There's nothin' goin' in or outta the game. It's like we been completely disconnected from NextWorld, yo."

"So what do we do?" Xen asks.

"We wait," Ekko says.

"For what?" Xen asks, but I don't need Ekko to answer him.

"The scheduled reboot of the game world," I say. Then I turn to Fantom and ask, "You think that will log us out?"

Fantom nods. "It should."

"It won't," Cyron says in little more than a whisper.

"Stop bein' so pessimistic, yo," Fantom says. "You ain't knowin' what's gonna happen."

"So we just wait for this reboot?" Xen asks.

"We're safe as long as we're in here," Ekko says.

"Okay," Xen says without any real conviction, but happy that someone has an answer for him.

He sits down against the far wall, trying not to look at the mangled avatar lying on the floor. I step toward Klok and toss my trench coat over the top of him, concealing the disturbing mess. After the sheer amount of violence I've seen in NextWorld, it's surprising that this simple image can still shake me, but it's because I know what it means for the player in the real world. I hate to admit it, but I feel something for him. It just might be the first time I've ever felt sympathy for another player.

00010011

The boredom is twisting my insides. The four blank, steel walls of the equipment shop seem to be closing in on me, and the already small room feels like it's shrinking as the game clock progresses.

It's not so bad at first. I'm at least interested when the group trades stories of their quests. I pay close attention to what the others are saying, hoping to take note of any information that I can about the higher level objectives so that I might have an advantage when I try to complete them in the future. As the hours drag on, we even reveal our inventories to each other, showing off our magical items and upgrades. I'm genuinely enthralled by what everyone has to say.

But as the morning draws closer, we run out of game talk. There simply isn't anything else to say. The group members start talking about the real world, and my attention drifts away. At first I try to act like I care. I nod, and smile, and force a laugh when the group laughs, but I'm not paying attention. Fantom talks about the classes she signed up for, but I don't listen to enough of what she says to even know what major she chose. Xen talks about Omniversalism and the new love in his life, but I've heard it all before. By the time it's Ekko's turn, I'm ready to pull out my virtual hair.

"Are you in DOTedu?" Fantom asks Ekko.

Ekko seems hesitant, rocking his wooden body back and forth as he contemplates how to answer. I want to scream across the room at him and tell him to stop pretending that what he's going to say is that important. I want to tell him how little I care. I want him to know how insignificant his life is, just like the rest of us.

"I'm not actually this young," he says. "Not in the real world."

The information is only slightly more interesting than I suspected. I'm wondering how weird this guy must be to design his avatar to look so young. I'm hoping he's not into anything *too* creepy. The fact intrigues the rest of the group, and they lean forward to hear more.

"This account belonged to my son. He..." Ekko pauses, sucking air into his wooden mouth to try to stop from whimpering. His image blinks in and out a few times before he continues. "He passed away last year. After I lost him, I was really... I didn't know what to do with myself anymore. I started using his avatar to play the same games in DOTfun that he used to play and... I guess it's my way of remembering him. He used to play these games so much. I guess I'm trying to let him keep playing."

"So what's with the voice masking?" I ask, and Xen elbows me, giving me a dirty look. "What? It's weird. He makes himself sound like a little kid, but he's speaking old Mandarin."

Everyone is glaring at me, except Cyren.

"So what, yo?" Fantom says. "We all change ourselves. One way or another."

"No," Ekko says. "He's right. It's probably weird. And I'm sorry if anyone feels like I was lying to them, but it's easier than having to tell everyone this story when they hear my real voice coming out of the mouth of this avatar. It's not a story I'd want to relive every time I group with new people."

I bite my tongue, reminding myself that it's easier not to interact at all. There was no reason to say anything, and now everyone thinks I'm a jerk for asking.

"That makes sense," Fantom says. "I ain't gonna blame you, Ekko. I'm sure your son would be proud of what you're accomplishin' with his avatar, yo."

Ekko selects a few things from his menu and says, "Is this better?" with his own adult voice coming from his avatar's mouth.

The whole thing is weird, no matter what voice he's using, but I keep my thoughts to myself. I stand up from the circle and pace around the room.

"What about you, Arkade?" Ekko asks when he sees me move.

I stop myself from speaking. I want to tell him that what he sees is what he gets, that this is really who I am. I don't have a quaint story about a dead son to justify my avatar's look. I stole the image from an old video-cast. I'm a gamer, pure and simple. My avatar is who I am, not that body in the real world. I try to think of the most diplomatic way to say what I want to say, but diplomacy makes me feel like my father, and I hate that.

"There isn't much to tell. I'm just a kid."

Everyone waits for me to continue, but my body language makes it apparent that they're waiting for nothing.

"Where's your tower?" Ekko asks, trying to continue the conversation with me.

"Look... I'm sorry, okay? I just don't feel like sharing."

"*Kade*..." Xen says my name in a long, drawn out way that sounds whiny.

"No," Ekko says. "It's okay, son. If you don't want to talk, you don't have to."

I barely hear Fantom say under her breath, "He could try actin' normal, yo."

I'm about to lash out at her, spitting questions at her, asking her what "normal" even means, but Ekko starts talking again, cutting off my impending tirade.

"What about you, Cyren?"

She barely smiles, and says with a whisper, "I don't know."

I can feel her anxiety from across the room. All the eyes on her feel like weights. I can see it in her shoulders, in the way she shifts her position. I can tell all this because I've felt it myself. She looks at me, and I feel a strange need to save her from the awkwardness, but I don't know how. I can barely save myself.

"You must have a story," Xen says, thinking he's being supportive. "Omniversalism teaches us to open our ears when someone talks, because everyone has a story."

Cyren keeps looking at the floor. She uses her thumb to rub a smudge off her buckled, leather boot. The silence drags on, almost to a breaking point.

"Look at the time," Fantom says, cutting the tension. "Reboot in ten minutes, yo."

"The game should have announced it," I say. "We got a thirty-minute warning yesterday."

"It's not going to reboot," Cyren mumbles.

Fantom shakes her head defiantly. "Stop sayin' that."

I hear more than anger in her voice. It almost sounds like fear, but her face is still covered in that emotionless white paint. She's gesturing in the air with everyone else. We're all checking different screens, hoping that some kind of message has popped up while we've been waiting. Only Cyren continues to sit on the floor, unmoving. I almost admire her carelessness about what happens. I envy her assuredness, even if it's pessimistic. No matter how bleak, in her mind, she knows what's going to happen. It's the not knowing that's killing the rest of us.

The game clock ticks down, and I can feel us holding our collective breath. I close my eyes and count the last seconds in my head, waiting for anything. I'm not ready, mentally, but I'm out of time. I don't know what's going to happen, even if the reboot occurs. It's far from a foolproof plan. It could still throw us into a coma, launching us all into an unconscious limbo.

Five.

Four.

Three.

Two.

One.

And time keeps moving. I open one eye and see the equipment shop, with everyone still standing around me. I open the other eye as everyone else lets out their held breath, their bodies deflating with the release. We look defeated, but no one knows what to say.

We all want to express our disappointment, but no one knows how. Not sufficiently.

Fantom spits out a single curse word, and it feels better than anything I could have expressed.

I lean my back against the steel wall and let myself slide down, inch by inch, until I land with a thud on the floor. The rest of the group follows suit, collapsing in their own ways. Everyone is so overwhelmed that they no longer contain the physical or mental energy required to keep themselves standing. Only Cyren remains unchanged by the news. Her emptiness continues.

00010100

I can barely lift my hand to open a screen in front of me. My energy is almost completely depleted. Not only am I mentally worn out and depressed, but I'm physically tired. It wouldn't be the first time I slept while I was logged in, but it never equals a good night's rest. I halfheartedly swipe through my character profile, quest screen, and map, but there's nothing new.

"What are we going to do?" Xen asks, but the way he says it, I'm not sure if he's asking us, or himself.

I want to say something that will comfort him, but it isn't in me. I wait, hoping someone else has more experience with that kind of thing.

"Don't worry, son. We'll survive," Ekko says. "My sister works with the emergency services in Old Mongolia. She takes care of all sorts of situations, including things like this."

"Things like *this*?" I say with a slightly skeptical laugh.

"Sure," Ekko says, like he doesn't recognize my sarcasm. "If someone doesn't log-out from NextWorld for thirty-six hours, there's a series of steps they're trained to complete. They try to contact the user online. If that doesn't work, they request a forced log-out from the NextWorld servers. If that doesn't work, they track their signal and send someone to their tower room. Of course, nobody wants them to do a cold shutdown with the danger it poses to your nanomachines, so in the worst case scenario, they have emergency E-Womb devices to supply all the necessary life-support you could need."

Xen's eyes light up as he says, "Really?"

"Of course," Ekko says. "And that's just here in Old Mongolia. We aren't exactly on the cutting edge. Don't worry about your health. I'm more worried about keeping my sanity in this little room. Boredom is going to be our biggest enemy."

"That's a relief," Xen says. "I was sitting here trying to remember when my last vitapaste consumption was… and not to be gross or anything, but I can't remember when I last used the toilet."

Ekko gives us all this very fatherly, comforting smile, which is weird coming from his wooden little boy avatar. His image flickers.

"You're going to feel hungry, son. There's no doubt about that. Thirty-six hours is a long time to go without food. But no one is going to die. You can be sure of that. Not only would DOTgov not allow there to be any risk involved in using NextWorld, but neither would the creators of *DangerWar*. All we have to do is wait."

I have to admit, the information does make me feel better. Knowing there isn't a time limit on my existence is good news. When I look around at everyone's response, Cyren is still lost inside herself, her own thoughts consuming her expressions. But it's Fantom that surprises me. I can actually see her avatar's hands shaking in front of her. Her eyes are shifting back and forth. She looks nervous, and the fact that I can see it in her normally emotionless face makes me realize how serious it is. Unsurprisingly, Xen notices too, and he's the one who reaches out to her.

"Are you okay?" he asks in a hushed tone, meaning to share the question with only her, but in the small size of the room, we can all hear.

She glances up at him, then away just as quickly. "Yeah," she says unconvincingly. When she sees that we're all looking at her, she replies, "I'm fine, yo."

Ekko reaches out to her. I catch myself wanting to laugh. If I know Fantom at all, I know she isn't going to respond to physical affection. Whatever is bothering her, lame attempts at comfort aren't going to help, especially when his hand is shifting from left to right randomly.

"There's no need to worry," Ekko says.

She looks up at him and says, "For me there is."

"There is?" Xen asks.

Fantom looks over at him and recognizes the worry that's spreading across his face. She lets out a long, annoyed sigh and rubs her forehead.

"Look," she says, "it ain't nothin' *you* gotta worry about. Just... forget it, okay?"

Xen keeps staring at her with that gentle look on his face. I'm watching them both, amazed at the strangeness of human interaction.

"Fantom... if there's something bothering you, you can talk to us about it. We're a group now. Omniversalism teaches us that no one can handle everything on their own."

I try not to take what he says personally, and my mind is already arguing against his statement, defending my own predilections toward solo play, but Fantom takes what he says to heart.

"Sorry, I... I just don't think I can be sittin' round here waitin', yo."

The statement is surprising. I can't believe she'd risk going outside just because she's bored.

"What would make you go back out into *that?*" Ekko asks.

She sucks in a lungful of air, hesitating to speak anymore, but she lets out the breath and says, "The things you're talkin' about, the systems they got in place to make sure no one's gonna be dien' if they stay logged in too long... They ain't gonna be workin' for me."

Ekko smiles and says, "I know you're worried, kiddo, but you shouldn't be. All of us will be safe. DOTgov will protect us."

Fantom shakes her head, and I can hear her crying. She didn't design her avatar to display tears, but her whimpers are coming through the audio.

"Fantom?" Xen says her name like he's questioning her panic.

She clenches her fist and groans, obviously annoyed with her own emotional breakdown. She takes another deep breath and tries to collect herself.

"What are you worried about?" Ekko asks.

"They ain't gonna find me, yo."

"Of course they are," Ekko says. "They're tracking everyone's avatar. They know exactly what tower room your body is in right now. They'll send some worker like my sister, and they'll take care of you and make sure nothing happens to you."

"You ain't understandin'," Fantom says, covering her face. "They ain't gonna find me, cause they ain't trackin' me."

"You're just panicking," I say, already annoyed by the conversation.

"Shut up!" she yells at me, the sound of her whimpering cutting through the audio again.

"Fantom, he's right," Ekko says. "You're just scared—"

"Which Omniversalism teaches us is perfectly normal," Xen injects.

"Sure," Ekko says. "Sure it's normal. But trust me, they track everybody."

Fantom looks at him with piercing eyes. "Not everybody, yo."

Ekko nods, and with a very serious tone he says, "Yes. Everybody. Why would you think you'd be any different?"

Fantom shakes her head and says, "Because DOTgov don't really care much for hackers."

00010101

I look at Ekko's wooden face, and I can tell he's trying to hide his reaction to Fantom's revelation. He keeps staring at her, his image flickering back and forth.

"You're a hacker?" he asks, his voice dropping away from his usual comforting tone.

Fantom can't make eye contact as she says, "Yeah. Sort of."

"What does that mean?" I ask with more urgency than her answer is giving.

She glares at me for a second, then says, "It's complicated, yo. I got into hackin' when I wasn't accepted into any universities. I'd been applyin' forever, but no one was even takin' a glance at my application. And without a degree, I ain't really got a lot of choices. I didn't wanna be a wage slave and just be workin' to pay for my tower room and my daily dose of vitapaste. So I was realizin' that my only other option was to do some research and learn some skills that could allow me to get the things I need to survive."

"I still don't understand," Xen says, looking confusedly at Fantom. "Where did you learn how to hack?"

"Hackin' ain't somethin' you're gonna be learnin' from watchin' no video-cast tutorial. Any info bout hackin' in

NextWorld is classified under cyberterrorism and they delete it instantly. You can't just be learnin' it. You gotta find someone to teach you."

"I still don't understand," Xen says. "How does hacking let you live in a tower room without having a job? Are you stealing credits?"

I find Xen's naivete embarrassing, but I keep my mouth shut and let Fantom explain it to him.

"I ain't no thief, yo. And this ain't about bein' a slacker or not wantin' a job either. I was only doin' this so the higher ranks of DOTedu would accept me, and then maybe I'd have a real chance of gettin' a degree. Then I could get a real job, somethin' that don't involve me crawlin' round air ducts or cleanin' out sewer blockages. I'm wantin' to design avatars or somethin'. I'm wantin' to use my brain, yo. But that wasn't gonna happen. My parents ended their partnership when I was really young, and my tower room is in the old North American territories. You got any idea how difficult it is convincin' the university to accept North Americans?"

"That's just leftover nonsense from the unification," Xen says with a solemn tone, shaking his head with disappointment. "Omniversalism teaches us that all people are equal, no matter where on the planet they might be located."

"Yeah, well, racism is still existin', yo. And I'm livin' with it."

She's right. The North Americans were the last to join the Global Government. I always admired them for their stubbornness, hence my old West cowboy avatar, but most people still look down on them. They slowed progression and a lot of people died in the rebellion. It's not something I've ever understood, blaming the current generation for the past generation's mistakes. It all happened before I was even born. But I've heard my father use old racist terms like "Northie" and "Yanker."

"I'm learnin' how to hack so I can be rewritin' my files and givin' myself a new identity. I'm gonna live my life the way I always wanted." Fantom smiles a bit. Then her face returns to the normally cold, vacant stare. "You can be judgin' me all you want, but just so you know, I ain't plannin' on usin' my hackin' skills for nothin' else. I coulda just transferred credits into my bank account or just be givin' myself the job I wanted. But I didn't. All I was doin' was evenin' the playin' field. I was givin' myself opportunities... opportunities that ain't available to me just cause I'm in the wrong part of the real world."

"Does this game qualify as one of those opportunities?" I ask.

She rolls her eyes. "I ain't played one of these games for years, yo. My brother was always playin' them, but he'd get so angry with me cause I was always better than him, no matter how long he spent practicin'. And yeah, now here I am playin' again, but that's only cause my partner dumped me, and I was sittin' round my tower room feelin' sorry for myself. An old hacker buddy sent me a message showin' me how to open a backdoor into the beta test. It was just supposed to be a distraction, somethin' to keep my mind off life for a while."

"So not only are you hacked into NextWorld, but then you doubled up and hacked into *DangerWar 2*?"

Fantom nods, but she doesn't make eye contact.

"And now the authorities are going to think you live somewhere else," Ekko says. "They have no idea your body is lying in an E-Womb somewhere in old North America."

"I'm reroutin' the input through a thousand different towers, yo. Even if they're tryin' to backtrack the signal, it'd take them weeks, maybe months, to find me."

None of us say anything. We all know what her words mean. If we don't log out soon, Fantom is going to die. Whether it's dehydration or starvation, she's going to die.

Ekko leans forward and wraps his wooden arms around her kimono. With Ekko touching her, his lag causes them both to flicker. Cyren looks up at me, and I shrug my shoulders. Neither of us join them. I can tell she's just as uncomfortable with the emotional expression as I am.

"I'll help you," Ekko says.

Fantom looks at him and smiles, her bottom lip appearing unsteady.

"I'll help you, too," Xen says.

"I ain't askin' either of you to do that, yo."

"You don't have to ask." Xen holds out his hand and Ekko grips it in a handshake. I see him select an invisible option in front of him.

I hear the announcer's voice say, "Xen has joined another group."

I find it all disturbing. Leave it to the gamer with something to prove to his dead son and the religious nut who probably wants to be a martyr to run off and play heroes. It's some romantic nonsense from a child's video-cast, and I'm not going to let their little role-playing game go any further.

"Hold on," I say. "How are you going to help her? What exactly are you going to do? You're acting like there's some kind of answer to our problem."

Xen gives me that disapproving look again, and Ekko considers my words, contemplating how to reply to my question, but it's Fantom who answers, and to my surprise, there's no anger in her voice.

"He's right. I'm willin' to go out there and look for whatever answers I can find cause I ain't havin' no other choice. But I ain't riskin' your lives too. I ain't gonna be the death of you, yo."

"There's no reason to speak of such things," Xen says, sounding pointlessly emotional. "We're here for you."

Ekko smiles and says, "We won't let you do this alone, kiddo."

The cliché reasoning is annoyingly meaningless when applied to the reality of our situation. I know I have to speak up, but it's Cyren who says something, and she takes the words right out of my mouth.

"You can't just go out there and wander around, hoping to stumble across a door with an exit sign. There's an entire game world of monsters trying to kill you. It's a hopeless battle, even if you had a destination."

"You can't be sure of that," Xen says.

"Yes she can!" I yell. "Stop acting like your good intentions will be enough to save her. All the kindness in your heart isn't going to protect you from a game world gone mad. Your Omniversalist teachings aren't going to help you."

Xen looks genuinely hurt. His face looks like I physically attacked him. He actually touches his chest and leans away from me.

Ekko frowns. "Do you have a better plan, son?"

"Me?" I ask, thinking the question is ridiculous. "Of course not. That's my point. There *is* no plan."

Ekko shakes his head, the image shifting back and forth. "It's easy to tell someone they're wrong. It's easy to point out errors. What's harder is telling someone how to do it right. The really difficult part is showing someone a better idea."

"The better idea is to stay here," Cyren says. "We've already established that."

"Thank you!" I say, finally feeling like someone is on my side.

Fantom shakes her head and says, "That ain't the best plan for me, yo."

"Wait a minute. What about your back door?" Ekko asks. "Can't you use that to get out of the game? Could we all use it?"

Fantom shakes her head. "We could've, but…" She almost looks bashful continuing her answer. "It… it ain't there. The last time I logged in, it disappeared. I didn't think much of it at the time. I was just figurin' I messed somethin' up in the code. I normally only used it to log in so I wasn't worried about it. It was stupid. I should've—"

"There was no way to know this would happen."

She shrugs. "Maybe there was. Maybe there wasn't. Don't matter no more. I gotta figure out what to do now."

"But you're assuming they aren't going to fix this problem in the next hour," I say. "Or even the next day. You're willing to get your avatar killed and put yourself in a coma, just because you aren't being patient enough."

Fantom grits her teeth and says, "I ain't got the luxury of patience, yo."

00010110

I want to argue with Fantom. I want her to just stay where she is, but then I realize it's because I don't want to feel guilty. I want everyone to stay inside where it's safe, because *I* want to stay inside where it's safe. I feel horrible as soon as I realize this, and I go into a mode of internal justification. I try to use logic to argue against myself, but my defensiveness is failing me.

"If we had reached a higher level, this probably wouldn't be such an issue," Ekko says.

"We're probably some of the highest level players there are. There ain't no scoreboard, so we can't be sure, but I ain't imaginin' anyone levelin' much faster than us."

"I met a player who was much higher level than you. He attacked me when I first entered the game." I only say it to shove it in her face that she isn't the best player out there.

Everyone turns to look at me, but it's Fantom who asks, "He was a higher level than us when you started?"

I shrug and smugly say, "A *lot* higher."

"How *much* higher?"

I smile. "He was level 72 when he attacked me, so who knows what he's at now."

The look on Ekko's wooden face says that he doesn't believe me. Xen doesn't realize the weight of this information. Cyren looks frightened by what I'm saying, probably already acknowledging to herself what this could mean. Fantom just looks stunned.

"You serious, yo?"

I nod.

"You remember his name?"

I shrug and say, "Sure. I made a mental note because it was such an unfair fight. I wanted to make sure to find him once I was a higher level, so I could give him a little payback."

"You should let that kind of thing go, Kade. Omniversalism teaches us to let the actions of others flow off our shoulders like water."

Fantom jumps off the floor and lands on her feet, rushing to the holographic screen. She scrolls through the options and opens the search screen.

"What are you doing?" Ekko asks.

Fantom keeps typing in different words, searching for something in particular. "I noticed somethin' before in the shoppin' lists. I didn't think much of it. It was in the PvP items. Seemed sorta pointless til now."

I step up behind her, interested again in the conversation. We're talking about the game again. I look over her shoulder and watch her scan through the nearly endless list.

"What was it?"

"A wrist compass, yo."

I glance at Ekko, and he just shrugs back at me. Xen looks just as confused.

Cyren is the only one who stands up and joins us at the screen. "You're talking about the player-tracker."

Fantom smiles and nods at Cyren.

"The what?" I ask, hoping someone is going to fill the rest of us in on their secret information.

Cyren leans behind Fantom so she can see me as she says, "It's an item that lets you track the whereabouts of specific players. It's expensive. It was designed for a player who wants to seek revenge against another player."

Fantom smiles and says, "Surprised you ain't heard of it, Cowboy."

"Very funny," I say. "So you want to use this to track down the high level player? And then what?"

She glances at me as she taps the "Confirm Purchase" button and says, "Hopefully he'll be tellin' me that, yo."

"Just because he's a higher level than us doesn't mean he has any idea of how to log-out."

The compass appears on Fantom's forearm as she says, "Yeah, well, right now he's my best bet." She adjusts the wristband and asks, "So, what's his name?"

I sigh and mumble, "Grael."

She selects some things on a screen I can't see, then frowns and says, "This ain't gonna be easy, yo."

I huff out a breath and say, "No doubt."

"No," she says. "I mean, he's in a high level zone, yo. A *really* high level zone."

"Of course," I say with a groan.

Xen gives me that look again and turns back toward Fantom. "Where is he at?"

"Up in the mountain zone."

"The mountain zone?" I say, my words breaking. "You mean the zone with that dragon flying around?"

"That's suicide," Cyren says. "You can't go there."

Fantom looks at the floor and says, "I ain't got no choice, yo." Then she looks up at all of us and says, "But *you* do. I ain't askin' you to be riskin' yourselves."

Xen smiles. "I already told you that I'm coming with you."

I slap my forehead with my palm.

Cyren gives me a worried glance. I raise my hands in the air as if to say, "I don't know what to do."

Her head droops between her shoulders, and she looks like something pulls her toward Fantom. "I told you I would protect you when I joined the group, and I meant it. If you're going out there, I've got your back."

And with that, I lose my last hope. The whole group is staring at me. They're waiting for my response. All of them have the same look in their eyes. It's that pathetic begging, that desperate longing for my compliance. Xen holds out his hand.

I look around the blank room and try to imagine what I'd do by myself, all alone. At least outside I can play the game. I sigh, heavier than I've ever sighed before, because now the fear of boredom is going to be the death of me.

"I'll go," I say, gripping Xen's hand and selecting the option to join their group, "but you're buying me some new gear."

00010111

"Spend every last Koin you've got," I say as the group purchases as many explosives, special munitions, and armor upgrades as our avatars can carry. "Who knows when we'll even be near another equipment shop."

When I notice that Cyren isn't buying anything, she assures me that she already maxed out her character. She tells me that she's a weapon-user, but when I ask her what weapon she chose, she just holds up her fist.

"Cyren is her own weapon, yo," Fantom says with a devilish grin.

Her strength stirs something deep within me. The feelings I have when I look at her buckled leather outfit confuse me. Girls are too much of a distraction. I don't lose myself in the thoughts because I know what that does to people. I only have to look at Xen.

I feel the need to point out to the group that Xen is our weak link, which doesn't offend him enough. He accepts the fact, and it doesn't bother him that I bring it up in front of the group.

"I'm only level 2," he says. "I think I'm close to leveling though."

"No worries, yo," Fantom says. "We'll be keepin' an eye on you."

"He's going to die," I say. "Or *we* will, trying to keep him alive."

"Arkade is right," Cyren says. "It'd be better for him to stay here, where we know he's safe."

Xen's voice remains calm and peaceful. "That isn't going to happen. I'm coming with you. Omniversalism teaches us to be brave, even in the face of imminent failure."

I start to argue more, but Fantom interjects. "It'll be fine, yo. With the amount of NPCs we're gonna have to kill, our group will be power-levelin' him. He'll be catchin' up faster than you think."

I can tell Cyren is still worried. I feel an urge to reach out and touch her shoulder. I want to comfort her and tell her I'm on her side, but I catch my thoughts and keep my hands to myself. Both of them.

"Are we ready for this?" Ekko says, then his image shakes and blinks, which fills me with anything but confidence.

I grab my trench coat off the mangled avatar of their former group member, Klok. "Are we just leaving him here?"

Fantom looks down at him and says, "There ain't no point in tryin' to save his avatar. It's too late for that. His real body is what we're worried 'bout now. If everythin' goes accordin' to plan, and we figure out a way to log-out, maybe we can still save him."

I feel better with my coat on, like I'm Arkade again, the same player who ran circles around my enemies in the original *DangerWar*. I adjust my cowboy hat and step over Klok's avatar.

Fantom steps up to the main door and says, "When Arkade opens this, we need to be ready for the worst. There could be an entire army out there waitin' for us. And it ain't gonna be just the low level NPCs. I'm sure the other NPCs have joined them by now. We could be facin'—"

"Anything," Cyren says, her voice still quiet, which only adds to the ominous feeling.

"She's right, yo," Fantom says, nodding at her.

"We can't attack from inside," I say.

"But they can't attack us, either," Ekko says.

"We need to be movin' fast," Fantom says. "We need to be gettin' out and attackin' before they can react. They ain't gonna be expectin' us and that's gonna be our only advantage."

"Move, shoot, and find a vehicle," I say matter-of-factly. "Our safest bet is to drive as fast as we can North, toward the mountains."

"Do you think your car will still be out there?" Xen asks.

"It ain't gonna matter," Fantom says. "That thing was so full of bullet holes, it was barely runnin' when we got here. And even if it does still run, we were hardly fittin' Cyren and Ekko in the back seat. There ain't no way we can all be usin' it now."

"If you can, find something big," I say. "Something that can take some hits."

Fantom adds, "And be killin' as many of those things as you can on the way, yo."

No one verbally agrees, but we all summon our weapons and aim them toward the door. Fantom stands in front, her shield glowing on her arm, hoping to protect us from the first wave of attacks. I reach out and touch the option to open the reinforced door and watch it slide upward.

I try to consume everything I'm looking at as the group rushes into the street. There's two cars with flames painted on the hood and small green-skinned men sitting inside with huge lower jaws and crooked teeth protruding over their upper lips. They're parked nose to nose, blocking the street in front of the equipment shop. I lift my guns, ready to fill the windshields with explosive rounds, but Ekko beats me to it. The muzzle of his rifle pops repeatedly and the green-skinned monsters inside the car shake as their bodies fill with bullets. His wooden avatar spins and pumps the other car full of bullets. Sparks fly from the few rounds that hit the hood before the windshield shatters, and the monsters inside slump forward.

I turn to the right, following the group and bringing up the rear. I'm watching behind us, but the street looks fairly empty. When I spin forward, I see a delivery truck parked only half a block away. The back of the truck is opening, and I see more of the green-skinned men climbing out of it. They're only half my size, but all of them are wearing armor and carrying automatic rifles.

"Goblins!" Cyren screams.

Fantom is already zipping across the street, and in a flash of light she slices the first goblin in half with her gigantic sword. As soon as the small body falls, the goblin behind him unloads a clip into her chest. The blast from the gun launches her into the air, and she lands flat on her back.

Xen tosses his small fireballs, but I shove him to the side and fire both of my pistols. My explosive rounds tear the goblin apart, even with his armor, but more of the creatures pour out of the door. I hold my fire, not wanting to damage the van. My brain has already kicked into overdrive, imagining our luck if we can all get inside a truck that size.

Cyren dodges some gunfire from another goblin, then flips across the street. Bullets zip past her body, and before they unload an entire magazine, she's already positioning herself next to three of them, slamming the flat of her palm into the face of the closest one. She ducks down as another rifle turns toward her. She spins, extending her leg to trip the goblin. She knocks his feet out from underneath him, and her elbow lands on his ribcage as he slams against the street.

The last of the three goblins slams the butt of his rifle into the back of her head. He yells something at her, but I can't hear it. Ekko is unloading his rifle right next to me, and the goblin blows apart into a few large pieces.

"Get inside!" I yell, pointing at the truck and turning around to check behind us again.

I see two more cars come squealing around the corner. Xen stops next to me, ready to fight, but I shove him toward the truck.

"Move!"

He reluctantly extinguishes the green fireball in his hands, and follows Ekko into the back of the truck. I pull both triggers, pecking away at the approaching cars. Finally, one of my explosive rounds punctures the hood of the car, and the engine catches on fire. The car careens to the left and slams into the front of a building. The other car keeps coming at me, and I realize they aren't going to stop. They're trying to run me down. I glance over my shoulder and see Cyren climbing in the back of the truck. I don't see Fantom, so I can only assume she's inside too. I keep stepping backward, toward the delivery truck, letting loose as many bullets as I can toward the car that's only building in speed.

Just as I'm about to give up firing and leap to the side, I see Fantom zip toward the car. She crouches down as it passes her, holding out her sword and slashing the front tire. The car squeals to the side, shoved to the left by the explosion of the wheel. It turns sideways, and I have a clear shot at the goblin driver through the side window. I see the pupils of his huge eyes as he sees my pistol raising at him. A single explosive round fires from my gun as the car slides past me, and I watch the NPC driver explode into a burst of flames. The car smashes into the building next to me, and the passenger goes flying through the windshield, mangling himself on the broken glass. I hear him release a series of painful moans, and I find the programming required to simulate that kind of anguish to be rather shocking.

That's when I realize that none of the NPCs are disappearing.

00011000

I'm staring at the writhing body in the shattered windshield, and it's only a hand grasping my arm that shocks me out of it. I spin around and see Fantom yanking me toward the delivery truck.

"Let's go!" she screams with annoyance. "We ain't got time to be admirin' the graphics, yo."

My brain returns to the state of fast-forward that I prefer, and I find myself already running toward the driver's door. As soon as I open it, Fantom is shoving herself past me, climbing up toward the steering wheel.

"I always drive, yo," she says without a hint of laughter.

I'm about to argue, but I hear the sound of gunfire. I run around the front of the truck and the engine starts. Fantom is stomping on the gas pedal before I'm inside. I yank my door shut as the delivery truck lurches forward.

"We've got more cars behind us," Ekko yells, his face pressed up against the tiny windows in the back doors.

Gripping the steering wheel with both hands, Fantom says, "I'm more worried 'bout what's in front of us."

I peer out the windshield and see a wall of dead NPC corpses blocking the street. Aliens, werewolves, zombies, and other things I don't recognize. All the dead bodies from last night are still lying there, heaped on top of each other. Without a reboot, nothing is resetting.

"Turn around!" Xen yells.

"I can make it, yo," Fantom says as she accelerates.

The truck plows through the corpses, knocking the lifeless NPCs to the side. The vehicle bounces around as it runs over a few of the bodies, but the truck is heavy and keeps itself stable. Unfortunately, we also make a clear path for the other cars to follow us.

"Okay," I say, "open those doors and let loose."

Cyren throws open one of the back doors, and I see the cars closing in on the truck. Ekko drops to one knee and tilts his rifle upward. He reaches forward and grabs onto one of the upgrades to his obscenely large gun. I hear a pop of air and a small, round grenade goes spinning into the air. It lands on the hood with painted flames and explodes, pushing the front of the car into the pavement and the vehicle flips end over end. I barely hear the Koins drop into my inventory.

"How we doin' back there?" Fantom asks as she wheels the truck around a corner.

I hear another grenade launch and the sound of an explosion ripping metal apart, so I smile and say, "We're doing okay, actually. These goblins must be low level."

"Good," she says through her clenched teeth. "Cause we're about to be havin' other problems, yo."

I look ahead of us and see two centaurs run out into an intersection. They're both holding humongous spears and they waste no time hurling them straight at the truck. Fantom does her best to turn the steering wheel in an attempt to dodge the attack, but she only manages to deflect one of the giant metal tips off the truck's side. The other spear sinks deep into our front grill. The engine sputters for a moment, but keeps moving us forward.

I watch as another set of spears appear in both of the creature's hands, so I lean my torso out of the window next to me, pointing both pistols straight at them. The explosive rounds slam into the centaurs, but they take the damage without flinching. I barely manage to slow them down.

"These things ain't from any quests we've seen," Fantom yells.

I keep unloading my pistols at them, hoping to at least distract them long enough for the truck to get past, but when we get less than twenty yards away, they both crouch down on the street. I see them plant the base of their spears in the ground to brace for impact, pointing the head upward, toward our approaching vehicle.

I slide back inside the truck and grab a hold of the steering wheel. Fantom screams at me, but I yank the wheel toward me, turning the heavy truck to the right. It's such a sharp turn that we tilt up on two wheels, drifting around the corner of the intersection and slamming our back end into one of the spears. I hear more metal tearing and a few screams from the back of the truck. Once we're going straight down the road again, I look in the back and see the giant spear sticking straight through one wall, the sharpened head only inches away from Xen's face.

"You okay?" I ask, but he only nods in reply.

I turn back around and look out the windshield, expecting more monsters to be descending on us, but I see a vacant street. Stores and restaurants line both sides of the four lane road, but everything looks empty. Cars are no longer sitting in the lots or next to the parking meters. No random civilians are wandering on the sidewalks.

Then we turn another corner.

There are craters in the street still smoldering from explosions and bullet holes mark the walls of buildings. I see a player's avatar stuck to a wall with arrows. An overturned tank rests in the middle of the road. It looks like a post-apocalyptic simulator.

"They're still on us," Ekko says, loading another grenade into his massive gun.

I look in my side mirror and see the two centaurs galloping down the street. Both of them are holding huge spears again, and despite their hooves, they're still gaining on us.

"I don't know if my grenades will even do anything to them," Ekko says, readying himself by the back doors.

My brain is spinning, trying to come up with a plan to stop them. If we can't kill them, we need to trap them, or at least slow them down enough to get away.

Cyren's eyes lock on mine. "Stop the truck."

It doesn't register at first, but before I can filter how to reply, she's opening the backdoor and leaping toward the enemies. She floats through the air for an impossible length of time, arms outstretched, catching the wind like the sail of a ship. Both centaurs hurl spears at her, but miss the moving target.

"Stop the truck!" everyone screams at once.

Cyren lands hard on one of the centaurs, and his horse legs fold underneath him. She rolls to the side, but is back on top of him before he can recover. She systematically grabs each leg, and with a powerful chop of her hand, breaks the bone.

The other centaur looks at our stopped truck, then back at his fallen companion, trying to decide what to do. He waits too long, and Cyren is leaping through the air again, this time wrapping her legs around the centaur's bare back.

Fantom watches the attack in the side mirror, and I hear her mumble to herself, "*Wow*."

"She's incredible," I say in agreement.

The centaur wheels around, trying to strike at Cyren, but she remains on his back, like an itch he can't scratch. Her hands wrap around his face. His fingers latch onto her forearms, trying to pry her grip away from his eyes, but she digs in deep.

The centaur screams. He bucks onto his hind legs, throwing Cyren to the ground, but it's too late. He's blind. His hands touch his face, then reach into the air, grasping for anything to give him stability. Cyren sidesteps around him and runs back to the truck, jumping through the back doors and slamming them shut behind her.

"Go," I say to Fantom.

I never take my eyes off Cyren. She looks bashful, but keeps glancing in my direction as Xen and Ekko congratulate her. I feel the urge to tell her how amazing that was. I want to tell her that her movements were unlike anything I've ever seen. I want to tell her that her body is the deadliest weapon in any game I've ever played. And I want to whisper all of this in her ear.

"Arkade."

Fantom says my name, and I shake off the strange urges I'm feeling. I look toward her, and she points out the window at a road sign that reads, "Highway."

00011001

Fantom wheels the truck onto the ramp and merges onto the wide roadway. The four lanes loop around the entire city in one huge circle. We head north, toward the mountain peaks rising above the rest of the game world. Debris, corpses, and abandoned vehicles litter all the lanes. Huge parts of the road are missing, bombed and destroyed by explosions.

"How long will this world last if there's no reboot?" I ask, but I think I'm only asking myself.

Cyren is next to me, looking over my shoulder and peering out the window with me. "They won't stop until everything else is dead. That's the only way this war will stop."

I turn and look at her. Her cheek is only inches from my face. "Is that what you think this is?"

She turns and looks at me. Now her lips are so close to me I can almost smell them. "I don't know what else you would call this."

"She's right," Fantom says. "It's like they declared war on us, yo."

"They?"

Fantom never takes her eyes off the road. "The NPCs. The game. Whatever. We're on one side and everythin' else is on the other."

"What about the civilian NPCs?" I ask. "We haven't seen any of them."

"Maybe they're hidin' like the players. These monster NPCs would kill them too."

Cyren points down the road. "There's something up ahead."

I squint my eyes, but I can't see anything. I'm about to ask, but as we drive closer I can make out a long black line that stretches across every lane. I lift the goggles off my neck and strap them around my eyes. The telescoping feature zooms down the lanes and I see the NPCs in high definition.

"It's a roadblock," I say.

We pass a road sign that reads, "Darkfyre Mountains – 2 km."

"They're blocking the zone entrance," Cyren says. "They're trying to keep us contained."

I adjust my goggles and zoom in closer, trying to examine the NPCs that pace back and forth. I see the glowing armor, signifying its magical properties, and they're all equipped with some sort of advanced submachine guns. When I see them spot our approach, they open their mouths wide and hiss. Behind each of their lips, I can see two long fangs.

"Vampires," I say, and I can feel the shudder run through everyone in the group.

"You sure?" Fantom asks.

"Those are high level NPCs," Cyren says. "They shouldn't be in a low level zone like the city."

"They also shouldn't be out during the day, but I don't think the NPCs are following a lot of rules anymore," Ekko says from behind me.

Cyren grabs onto my shoulder, and her fingers dig in as she says, "We need to turn around."

I pull the goggles off my face and look in her eyes. I speak in something a little over a whisper, caught in the intimacy of our closeness. "You don't think we can beat them?"

"They're too powerful."

"So were the centaurs," Fantom says, "and you managed to kill them, yo."

Cyren shakes her head, her face looking strained as she says, "I didn't kill them. I only… incapacitated them."

Fantom lets off the gas pedal and says, "So what are we supposed to do?"

I lift my goggles again and scan the road ahead of us. The exit ramp is only a short distance beyond the roadblock. It leads down to a gravel road that winds into the wooded hills that surround the mountains.

"Turn," I say, taking off the goggles.

Fantom looks at me with panicked confusion. "What're you talkin' bout? There's nowhere to be turnin'."

"Just turn!"

She looks at the cement barrier, blocking us from careening off the raised highway. Then she looks back at me. I give her a single nod of my head. She buckles her seat belt, and I do the same.

Cyren yells over her shoulder into the back of the truck when she realizes what we're planning to do. "Everyone hang on to something!"

The armored vampires pepper our truck with bullets, and Fantom cranks the wheel to the left. The tires squeal and we jump the divider between the four lanes. As soon as we land on the other side, Fantom presses down on the gas pedal as hard as she can.

"Here we go!" she yells, locking her elbows, and bracing herself against the steering wheel.

The delivery truck smashes into the short, cement wall. The impact throws me forward, and I watch hunks of gray rock go flying into the air. The view of the ground raises up into the windshield, and I feel us dropping. We're falling fast, and even though my Anti-Gravity Belt kicks in, pulling me against my seat belt, it grants me no advantage as the truck drags me with it. It's tilting forward too far, and I know we aren't going to land on our wheels. It only takes a few seconds before we hit the road below us, the front of the truck crushing into itself. The windshield shatters, and I feel the tiny specks of glass fly into my face. With a horrible noise, the truck tips to the right and lands hard, finally coming to a rest, lying on its side.

I blink a few times, trying to give my brain a moment to stop spinning. I hear moaning all around me. I see Cyren unbuckling Fantom from her seat belt.

Cyren looks at me and says, "Are you okay? You still with me?"

I nod.

"Help me get them out of the truck," she says. "Those vampires will be on us in no time."

I fumble with the latch on my own seat belt, but I eventually release myself and fall to the side. I crawl over my seat, into the back of the truck. Xen is curled up in the corner, unconscious, but Ekko is gone.

"Where's the wooden boy?" I groan.

The backdoor swings open, and I reach for my pistol, expecting the group of vampires to come rushing into the truck. Instead, I see Ekko.

"Time to go, kids," he says.

"How did you—"

He looks down, almost ashamed. "My lag. When we were falling, I shifted right through the truck." He looks up, back toward the overpass. "We need to go. Now."

I grab Xen by his loose, orange wrappings and rattle him around, yelling his name. His bald monk avatar doesn't open its eyes. The thought of his death fills my head and it almost paralyzes me. I realize my role. I immediately accept my guilt and the responsibility for him being in this world that wants him dead.

Ekko tries to help me lift Xen off the floor. Cyren and Fantom climb past us and crawl out the back doors.

"Hurry," Cyren says, holding the door for me as I drag Xen's body from the truck.

As soon as I'm in the street, I throw Xen's skinny avatar over my shoulder. "Let's move."

As we make our way from the truck and the highway, bullets crack the surrounding pavement. We all spin around and look up toward the spot in the overpass where our truck broke through the barrier. The squad of armored vampires hold submachine guns to their shoulders, the flare of their muzzles flashing. I feel rounds strike my leg, then my chest. My armor soaks up the damage.

"Run!" Fantom screams, using her magic ring to zip toward the gravel road that leads to the mountains.

I jog with the group, Ekko and Cyren moving faster than me. I feel more rounds strike my back as I run. One hits my ankle and trips me. My face plows into the ground, and Xen's body tumbles away from me. I roll onto my back, hearing the bullets striking the ground all around me. More hit me in the chest. I try to scramble away, but the bullets rain down, covering the entire area around me.

Something inside me tells me to close my eyes and wait for the inevitable, but I refuse to listen to it. I keep pushing my heels against the ground, shoving myself away from the gunfire. Rounds continue to pelt my body like a thousand tiny gnats that won't stop biting. I know my armor will only hold up for a few more seconds, then those shots will eat away at my endurance rating. After that, I'll see the red color of impending death.

Fantom steps over me. She raises her arm, and her energy shield appears. Ekko stands next to her, launching grenades in between emptying magazines of bullets at our attackers.

"Get up," I hear Cyren say behind me, and I feel her hands hook underneath my armpits.

The group came back for me. They're all risking their lives to make sure I don't lie down and die. I was reluctant to join them on this suicide mission, and here they are, turning around and running back for me without a second thought.

As soon as Cyren gets me on my feet, she runs to Xen, throwing him over her shoulder. I don't turn toward the vampires to look at them. Instead I follow Cyren up the gravel road, running as fast as I can. I only allow myself to glance backward once, to see if Ekko and Fantom are still with us. Thankfully, they are.

Ekko is covering our exit with his rifle, but the gunfire from the vampires fades away. I picture in my mind the armored men dropping from the overpass, their undead speed carrying them down the road after us. I imagine them tackling me to the ground and their fangs sinking into my neck. I imagine the endless dream that's about to become my life, the never-ending unconsciousness that my mind would fall into if my avatar were to die.

The end of thought.

The end of me.

I see Xen's eyes blink a few times as his head bounces against Cyren's back. The jostling wakes him up, but his head turns from side-to-side, trying to take in his surroundings.

"What, um, where are we?"

Cyren stops for a second when Xen starts to fidget and sets him down on his feet.

"Hey. Neat," he says with a smile. "I leveled. A lot."

I run up to him and grab him by his orange wrappings, yanking him with me, trying not to slow down.

"Keep moving," I yell. "There's no time for congratulations."

And that's when I hear Fantom yell from behind me, and she's yelling the words that at that moment I fear the most.

"They're chasin' us, yo!"

00011010

I see them, far down the road. Multiple black figures moving fast. Faster than us. They're zigzagging up the street, changing their formation constantly. They don't fire at us, but they're closing the gap. I don't have time to stop and look again. I face forward and run like everyone else. We're all running as fast as we can. It's all we can do. I hear the vampires hissing, even from this distance. The noise grows as they gain on us, and it sounds like a swarm of insects descending from the sky.

"We ain't gonna make it," Fantom says, and I think it's the first time I've heard her give up on our chances.

"We have to," Ekko says through his panting breath. "We *have* to."

"We can't outrun them," I say, pulling my revolvers from their holsters. "We have to make a stand."

"They'll tear us to pieces," Cyren says. "We can't fight them. It's over."

My brain is churning, trying to work out a strategy to stop them. I look at the forest ahead of us, and I wonder if we could lose them in the trees. But it's too far away. They'll be on us before we can reach it. If one of us was to sacrifice themselves, or if I injured one of the group members, I wonder if the others could make it while the vampires attacked the one straggler. But there's too many vampires. They outnumber us at least two-to-one. My head swells as I try to force out some kind of plan, any kind of plan, before I die.

Cyren looks just as panicked, and I can see her mind working as fast as my own. "Xen! Did you get the level 8 fire spell?"

"I sure did," he yells back, his hands bursting with the green flames.

Her eyes light up and she points at the vampires, yelling, "Use it!"

I see him stop running, and I know he's going to die. I wonder if Cyren is sacrificing my friend for the good of the group, and I realize that I agree with her decision. It makes me feel black inside. Empty. Like I'm missing something really important. Something that makes me human.

"Xen! Run!" Fantom screams, but she's already unsheathing her sword and powering up her shield.

"Your spells are too weak!" I yell, but he's not listening.

I see the black figures, now only fifty yards from us. They'll cover that distance in seconds. Xen waves his arms out in front of him, raising a wall of green fire from the ground. He points his arms high into the air, and the flames rise with his hands, reaching twenty, then thirty, then forty feet into the air.

I can barely see the armored vampires through the flickering light. They hiss and back away from the fire. The leader points to the sides, and I wait for them to simply make their way around the wall. Xen twirls his hands in a loop, and the wall of fire curls outward. The edges wrap themselves around the vampires, creating a circle to entrap them. The black-clad figures back themselves into each other, still hissing, but I hear fear in the noises they make. With another wiggle of his fingers, the flaming wall devours the vampires, engulfing their bodies until all that's left are piles of ashes.

"He got that spell at level 8?" I mumble to myself, looking down at my own revolver. "That's not really fair."

"That spell wouldn't cause much damage to you," Cyren explains as everyone else congratulates Xen. "But vampires have a weakness to fire. They can't touch it, no matter how low the damage rating is."

I find it impressive that she knows so much about the fire spells, even though she doesn't use magic. It just shows how good of a player she is, and how devoted to the game she is. She's pretty amazing.

"Let's move, people. I don't want to wait around for something else to find us," I yell as I continue my run up the road, not waiting for them to follow.

I hear their footsteps behind me, and within minutes we're at the edge of the forest. The gravel road shrinks to nothing more than a wide dirt trail, bumpy and overgrown. I slow when I see a wooden sign with the word "Danger!" crudely painted on it.

"We should stay on the trail," Ekko says, sounding like every other adult.

I shake my head. "Actually, we need to do the exact opposite."

Even Fantom looks at me, confused by my strategy. I let out a heavy breath before I try to explain my thought process.

"The trail is what the designers expect us to follow. That's where all the big, staged encounters are going to be waiting. If we wander through the trees and brush, we might move slower, but we'll probably only come across randomly-generated NPCs."

Ekko points behind us and says, "You might be right about staying on the road, but we've already seen that the game isn't following the normal rules anymore, son. We don't know what's going to happen for sure."

"It's easy to tell someone they're wrong," I say, quoting his own advice back to him. "The really difficult part is showing someone a better idea. Do you have a better idea, Ekko?"

He grits his wooden teeth in frustration with himself instead of anger with me and says, "No."

"Then let's go," I say, stomping my way through the thick grass surrounding the tree line. "We don't have time to argue."

Once we get under the canopy of trees, the foliage almost completely blocks out the sun. Thin streams of light break through here and there, but the darkness of the forest is spooky, even as we near midday. We try to stay as quiet as we can, but the brush makes it impossible. The crunching and thrashing of five players is hard to hide.

I'm not afraid of the sounds we're making. It's the other noises in the forest that worry me. Howls, screams, rattling, clicking, the fluttering of wings, and the gurgling of something unpleasant. It's always off in the distance, a few yards in front of us or behind us. I'm wondering if the sounds are actually coming from NPC monsters or if it's all part of the programming of the forest. Did the designers add these effects to make the trees seem even more haunted?

"We're movin' too slow," Fantom says in a hushed tone.

It's the first thing anyone has said since we entered the forest.

With a hesitant voice, Ekko says, "If we took the trail—"

"Then we'd be fighting something right now," I snap, "instead of moving forward."

Fantom's eyes shift around our surroundings. "At this rate, we ain't gonna be reachin' them mountains until sundown. And the climb is gonna take another day." She looks at the ground and says, "I don't know if I got that long, yo."

"The human body can last weeks without food," Cyren says. "Dehydration is your biggest worry."

The way she says it makes the idea sound cold, like she's reading the information from a medical journal. The look that Xen gives her is his standard disapproving gaze, but her unsympathetic nature stuns everyone. I can see her shrinking away from them, their judgmental looks beating her down until she glances at me, to see if the unspoken attack is coming from me as well.

That's when I realize that I empathize with Cyren more than I sympathize with Fantom. Cyren doesn't let emotion bog her down. She's letting Fantom know that her panic and worry is unfounded. She's using facts instead of pointless clichés about "hanging in there" or "staying strong." She's offering Fantom something of true substance.

"Cyren's right," I say, deflecting everyone's attention away from her. "And even dehydration will take you longer than a day or two. Your body might feel weak, but in here, that doesn't matter. Keep your mind focused, and you'll be fine."

Fantom pauses, considering what I just said, then nods her head and starts trudging through the brush again.

Cyren smiles at me. "Thank you," she whispers as she steps past me, touching my back with her leather-strapped hand for the briefest of moments.

00011011

My circle of thoughts about Cyren catches me in a hole I'm tumbling down. I wonder how alike we are. I remind myself how little I know about her. I try not to fill in the blanks, instead appreciating what I do know. I can relate to her social anxiety. We could both use a partner to fight that battle. I feel this urge to pull her next to me and watch her back. I've never felt that way toward another player. I watch my own back. She probably feels the same way that I do. She doesn't need my help.

I hear Fantom yell, and I look up from my lost gaze. It isn't a scream of shock or pain, but one of anger and frustration. I run when I see everyone else running. From the back of the group, I can't see what's happening. I rush through the overgrowth, pushing branches and leaves out of my way. Cyren is right in front of me, and walking in front of her is Ekko, who's following Xen. We all follow the trail that Fantom was hacking through the brush, clearing a semi-walkable path. I hear Xen let out a yell. I look past Cyren in time to see Ekko tossed into the air like the gravity just gave out on him. Cyren crouches down, and without her in front of me, I see Xen and Fantom missing as well. I spin on my heels, looking for the source of the attack. I look up, but all I see is movement. Every leaf is rustling and every branch is blowing in the wind.

Except there's no wind.

The trees are moving by themselves.

As soon as I realize this, a vine shoots down from the canopy of leaves above me and wraps around both of my legs. It pulls to the side and trips me, but the vine is pulling upward so quickly that before I can slam into the ground, it yanks me into the air. Branches whack me in the face as the vine hoists me fifty feet up into the trees. Leaves surround me, blocking my view, so I yell out for anyone who might hear me.

"Is anyone there?"

"I'm here," Ekko responds, sounding like he's only a few feet from me.

"Me too," Xen yells, but he sounds higher up and farther away.

"Cyren? Fantom?"

There's no reply. The vines tighten around my ankles, but I sense no other attack. I dangle there, feeling helpless.

"Can anyone get themselves free?" Xen asks.

I struggle to pull myself up to my ankles and slide my fingers under the coarse vine. I pull hard, but it won't budge.

"Right about now, I'm wishing I chose a knife as a weapon," Ekko says.

"No bayonet upgrade on that gun of yours?" I ask with a laugh.

"I'm going to try to burn this vine," Xen says.

"Be careful!" both Ekko and I yell out, but only Ekko follows it up with, "You're really high up, son. You don't want to fall from that height."

There's no reply, but over the chirping birds above me and the strange beastly sounds below me, I hear the faint crackle of fire. It only takes a few seconds, and then I hear a crashing sound and the loud yelling of Xen. The sounds of the skinny monk come closer, then pass me by, falling fast. I yell out his name, but it doesn't take long for him to hit the ground with a crash. I wait, saying nothing, holding my breath, trying to listen for any kind of noise coming from him. The seconds stretch on with nothing but silence. Then a faint groan rises from the ground.

"Xen! Are you okay?"

There's a long pause before he says, "Yeah." Another pause. "I think so."

I reach up again and struggle with my own vine, grunting with anger when I can't move them.

"Arkade?" I hear far off to my right. "Ekko?"

I recognize the voice as Fantom's, and I'm let down I that it isn't Cyren's voice instead. The leaves are rustling, but I hear a crashing of branches coming toward me. I brace myself for some kind of attack. I reach for my pistols, but my holsters are empty. I must have dropped them when the vines pulled me into the air. I cringe as the sound nears me, almost on top of me.

And then I see Fantom's face break through the covering of leaves. She's hanging on one branch, her toes are balancing on another. Her sword lashes out with two quick swipes. The first slices the main vine, the second slides between my ankles, cutting me free. I drop, but my Anti-Gravity Belt lets me float back down to the forest floor without harm.

I look up to say thank you, but Fantom isn't there. I hear her jumping through the leaves toward Ekko. When I land softly on the ground, Xen is resting against a rock, rubbing his legs. He smiles at me when he sees me, and I give him a small wave.

"I'm glad you're safe," he says.

"Have you seen Cyren?"

"I'm here," she says from behind me.

I turn around and take a step toward her, ready to hug her, but I stop myself. The gesture feels out of place. She gives me an anxious smile.

"How did you get free?" I ask.

"She was down here when I landed," Xen yells over to me.

The fact that he's answering for her annoys me, but I ask Cyren, "Weren't you attacked?"

She shrugs her shoulders and says, "I'm a little too strong for those vines to hold me."

"Oh," I say. "That's, uh, that's cool. That's really cool." My own fumbling embarrasses me, and I try to wrap it up. "I'm glad you're okay."

"You too," she says, and then she reaches out her hands, cradling both of my pistols. "I think you dropped these."

"Thanks. Thank you," I say, continuing to stumble over my words as I take my guns and put them back in their holsters.

She smiles at me and then steps past me, her shoulder brushing against my arm.

She's just so awesome.

Ekko and Fantom make their way back down the trees a few minutes later, slowly climbing down the trunk. Xen manages to get back on his feet, but I notice him walking with a limp, even though he's doing his best to hide it.

Ekko looks around and says, "We should keep moving, kids. That won't be the last random encounter."

"How much farther?" Xen asks, and I wonder if he even knows how to open his map screen.

"Let's get to the base of the mountain. We'll camp in the hills." I look at Xen's leg and say, "We all need rest."

We all agree silently and make our way through the rest of the forest, Fantom hacking through the brush with her sword. I bring up the rear again, keeping my eye on everyone with much more attention.

Every few minutes I notice Cyren glance back at me, but it's so brief I convince myself that I'm imagining it. I want to talk to her. Every time she looks at me, I try to think of something to say, some way to start the conversation. It would pass the time if nothing else. But I never think of anything good to say. Every sentence that pops into my head feels foreign and strange to me. Even with this player that I find so relatable, I can think of nothing relatable to share. So the group walks in silence, pushing our way through the thickness of the forest, waiting for the next attack. I let out a deep, relaxing breath at the thought of violence, because unlike talking, violence is something I know how to do.

00011100

The hills that break up the forest zone from the mountain zone are actually quite beautiful. Bright green grass blankets the rounded hills, making the landscape appear so perfect, it's like a child's animated video-cast. The sun is setting in the west, behind the lush jungle landscape far in the distance. A breeze blows through the valleys and the warmth in the air is lulling me into a state of calm detachment from the danger that lurks everywhere.

We're moving slower than I'd like, skirting around groups of jackal-headed tribesman and hairy beasts with jagged tusks jutting from their faces, but I know these higher level NPCs could easily kill us. We remain hidden, patiently waiting for the roaming packs to pass us.

By the time we make our way ten kilometers into the highlands, our feet are dragging behind us. We're all struggling, but no one is willing to be the one who asks to stop. I suck up my pride and do everyone a favor.

"We should camp," I say, and I hear a sigh of relief from nearly the entire group.

"Let's get to the top of this next hill, yo," Fantom says, pointing at the raised ground in front of us. "It'll be easier for us to keep watch."

"The NPCs will be able to see us easier, too," Ekko says. "We should stay in a valley."

"He's right," I say. "I hate to leave us without the advantage of higher ground, but we need to deal with the bonfire that comes attached to the camp item by default. We'll need to try to hide the light as much as possible."

Fantom stops, and I can see the weight drop off her shoulders as she realizes she doesn't need to move any further.

"Okay," she says. "Okay."

She drops onto the grass underneath her, crumpling more than sitting. She lets herself fall back so that she's lying down, staring up at the sky. A roar of a jet engine comes from above us, but when I look up, the plane is so high that all I can see is the contrail streaking behind it.

"That jet again," Xen says with a bit of jealousy in his voice. "Do you think that's a player?"

"It could be an NPC," I say.

Xen keeps staring up at the sky as he says, "This trip would have been a lot easier if we could just fly over these high level zones. Omniversalism teaches us that the direct path is always the best path."

I smile, seeing the envy in Xen's eyes that he'd probably never admit to having. His religious beliefs wouldn't allow him to accept something like jealousy, but I can tell he just wants to get his hands on that jet and find out what it feels like to fly.

"Who bought the camp item?" I ask, and Xen raises his hand.

With a few gestures he selects the item from his inventory and a single tent with a bonfire appears. It looks quaint. A few flat stumps appear next to the fire. Ekko sits down on one of them, leaning his rifle against his knee, always within reach.

"Only one tent?" Xen asks.

"According to the item description, it creates separate instances for anyone who enters the tent," I explain. "Each of us will have our own interior to sleep in."

"I'm hungry, yo," Fantom groans.

"Me too," Ekko says. "Which means my body hasn't been found yet."

Xen gestures through his screens and asks, "Aren't there food items in this game?"

"Don't bother," I say. "It will only make things worse. Tasting food is great, but without the substance it just makes you more hungry."

He nods, accepting the logic. "Then we should find some way to keep our mind off the hunger."

"Got any suggestions?" Ekko asks.

Xen gestures, looking through his screens. "There's no way to connect to any video or audio-casts, but maybe…"

He selects a few options, and I hear music. Light drums brush against each other for a few beats before a grinding bassline drops in, with harps and horns accentuating the vocals.

Ekko grabs his rifle with one hand and looks around us in a panic as he says, "Turn it down! You'll attract everything within earshot!"

"NPCs can't hear it," Cyren says.

"She's right," Xen says. "I can only broadcast to group members."

"How did you do that?"

Xen smiles big, and I see a glow in his face I haven't seen since Cherub Rock. "I can't access outside connections, but I can still open my own libraries. I store music in my avatar profile so I can listen to my own music if I'm at a club with a less-than-skilled DJ."

We all sit and listen to the song, which lasts for nearly fourteen minutes. No one says a word until Xen mixes into the second song.

"I can't believe how nice it is to just be sittin' here, listenin' to music," Fantom says.

Ekko smiles. "It feels normal."

"I'm just happy not to be killin' somethin', yo, or runnin' from somethin' tryin' to kill me."

The group seems to be relaxing as the songs mix from one to another. Only Cyren looks uneasy, unmoved by the music. I watch her and realize I'm not letting go of the tension in my mind either. There's a stress that keeps pushing me down, hanging on my brain like concrete and dragging me to the bottom.

"We need to figure out a schedule for keeping watch, kids," Ekko says.

I'm happy to get back to talking about the game, instead of letting the casual atmosphere strangle me. "Everyone should get some rest," I say. "I'll keep first watch."

Ekko stands up and slaps me on the shoulder as he walks past. The slap knocks me back more than I expect. Xen and Fantom thank me as they follow Ekko into the tent, one by one disappearing into their own personal interior as soon as they step through the flap. The fire in the center of the camp burns without ever needing to replace the wood, the flames always at the perfect height. I sit down on one of the stumps and see Cyren on the outskirts of the camp, staring up at the stars that are just beginning to twinkle.

"You should get some sleep," I call out to her.

There's a pause, then she turns her head and looks at me over her shoulder.

"I'm not tired."

I nod my head in agreement and say, "Me neither. I know I should be, but I think my adrenalin is still pumping. Today was…"

"Exciting," she finishes for me, turning and walking toward the fire.

I smile and say, "I wanted to say that, but," I look at the tent, making sure everyone is still inside before finishing my sentence, "I didn't want to make light of the situation. I mean, don't get me wrong, I'm as scared as everyone else, but—"

"It's okay," she says, sitting down on the stump across from me. "I understand. It's still a game, right? It'd be weird if it wasn't at least a little fun."

00011101

The fire makes Cyren's leather straps and metal buckles shine, reflecting the flames with an illuminated darkness. She looks like a black mirror.

I lean back, trying to look comfortable as I say, "It's nice to finally have some peace and quiet. I'm not used to grouping like this or being around other players for such a long period."

"You normally play solo?"

I nod. "I've just had… more success that way."

"You mean in the original game?"

"In every game."

We both watch the fire crackle in front of us.

"What about in the real world?"

I cringe.

"Do you have friends there?" she asks. "Family?"

I stare at the fire for a long time. I'm unsure of how to answer the question. I want to tell her the same thing I told the group during their little sharing session. I want to tell her that there's nothing to say. I want to tell her that the real world doesn't matter, and I don't want to talk about it, but I look up from the fire, into her eyes, and I see a longing to know. Her interest in me goes beyond the simple small talk people share to fill the silence.

I chip through the dam inside me. At first it's only a trickle that breaks through, but that soon becomes a flood.

"When I was younger, I lived with both of my parents in one of the family units. I think, even at that age, that I thought my mom was the one that wanted me. Most politicians don't have children. They think it's their duty to the government or something to not add to the population. I probably held that against him. I didn't want to be thankful to him just for allowing me to be born. And he was never really around. He was always campaigning in NextWorld. He'd come out of his E-Womb to eat and sleep, but that was it. My mom said he was spending time inside so that she and I could spend time together outside. But maybe she was right. Maybe he was just trying to give me a good childhood."

I rub my face, unsure if I want to continue. I know what I'm about to say, and the pain is already crushing me.

"I was ten when my Mom died. She had the first generation of nanomachines, before all the bugs were worked out. Her's malfunctioned. They didn't recognize a serious blood clot and never cleaned it out. She suffered a brain embolism. She died right in front of me."

I stop because in my brain, I can see it all. She's there again, right in front of me. Her eyes looking up at me. Empty.

"I sat with her for four hours before my dad logged out of NextWorld."

"Arkade, I…"

I can tell she doesn't know what else to say. I wish I could tell her she doesn't need to say anything. She doesn't need to feel responsible. I'm not looking for anyone to tell me they're sorry, or that it's all going to be okay. I just keep talking, pushing past it.

"It's been almost six years since that happened, and I've spent ninety-nine percent of that time in NextWorld. At first it was because I missed my dad. I figured if that was the reality where he was going to be, then I was going to be there too. But there was no place for a little boy in the DOTgov domain. So I wandered around DOTkid, like everyone my age, and that's where I met Xen. I think we bonded at that age because he was lonely too. He felt like no one understood him and his religion. I didn't understand it either, but I understood feeling misunderstood. Does that make sense?"

She nods and I can see in her eyes that she knows *exactly* what I'm talking about.

"As soon as the age verification allowed it, we both ventured to other domains. I went to DOTfun, and Xen went to DOTsoc. We were both looking for something else, something we couldn't find in DOTkid."

She smiles and says, "It sounds like you were both looking for companionship, just in different ways."

"I think you're right. We were reaching out in the only ways we knew how. Xen found what he was looking for... I didn't. I spent all of my student vouchers on games, yet I was still alone. I played with thousands, *millions* of other players, but I never grouped with anyone. I never saw anyone as my peer or socialized in any way. I ran around *DangerWar* killing anyone who crossed my path. I obliterated their avatars before they even had a chance to interact with me."

She smiles the saddest smile I've ever seen. I lose myself in the uniqueness of her design, intricate and defined. A dichotomy of edges and curves.

"But Xen..."

"Xen had to fight to be my friend," I say, still admitting more than I normally reveal. "He's kind of still fighting to be my friend. I mean, I've given him every reason *not* to be my friend. We were so young when we met. I'm not sure why he still tries so hard." I pause, a sadness falling over me. "But that's what makes him different, I guess. He's my friend because he always has been. I know I take it for granted. I don't appreciate it enough... not like I should, but that's because I don't understand it. We have nothing in common. We argue all the time. We spend our spare time doing completely different things. But maybe that's what makes our friendship stronger. Because despite all those differences, we still manage to care about each other."

"But you aren't comfortable around people, are you? Even him. I can see it."

The straightforward statement catches me off guard, and at the same time I love the fact that she isn't dancing around the subject.

"I just don't understand them. The way they interact. The choices they make. None of it makes sense to me. I prefer something logical. Something that has rules that aren't constantly broken or changed."

"I know what you mean."

"You do?"

She nods slowly and says, "I try to watch other people and… and to learn from them. I try to figure out what makes them tick, why they do the things they do. But I'm still at a loss."

"Me too!"

I think I sound too excited, but I can't help it. I've never shared those thoughts with anyone, much less had anyone agree with me. Something weightless fills me. The acceptance of another person has always been meaningless to me, yet here I am, warmed by her simple statement. Am I talking too much? I want to say more, I want to share more, but I have no idea how to do that. I have no idea how this works. Am I supposed to take things slowly, even though we're in a situation that borders on life and death? Do we have time to linger? Do we have time to be patient?

"Do you feel more comfortable logged in?" I ask. "Do you feel like this is where you belong? More than in the real world?"

Cyren looks up at the stars and says, "I feel like it doesn't matter whether you're logged in or out. It only matters where you are right now." She pauses and locks eyes with me. "Your mind is who you are. Your thoughts are what make you who you are. Your mind is your personality. Your mind is your self, your being. Your friend Xen might call it a soul, but does that exist in your brain or your body? I think that wherever your thoughts exist, *you* exist."

It's like she's reading my thoughts. It's like she's taking the words out of my brain and repeating them back to me. She's explaining exactly how I've been feeling for years and putting it more eloquently than I ever could.

"I agree. Completely."

"You do?" she says, looking at me with a strange sort of hope in her eyes.

"Absolutely. People think the real world is meaningful because that's where their body is." I beat my fist against my chest. "But this is a body too. This is just as real as that other body. My mind controls both. My mind is who I am."

She tries to hide her face, but the firelight doesn't let her. It's no longer sadness on her face. I know, because I'm feeling the same thing.

Something more powerful than my social awkwardness lifts me from the stump I'm sitting on and walks me around the fire. I sit down on the stump next to her hard leather body. She looks at me, no longer hiding.

I know now, that in all those moments in the past, it wasn't me that was awkward. It wasn't me that didn't fit in. It was the combination of me and the person I was with. It was our ill-fitting personalities, clashing against each other. Because here, now, I feel comfort. I feel like I'm exactly where I should be. I feel like I belong.

Next to her.

I reach out and touch her arm. It's cold, even though she's sitting so close to the heat of the flames. She leans against me, tilting her head to rest against my shoulder. I put my other arm around her and gently pull her closer. At first I think I'm holding her, but it doesn't take me long to realize the truth: we're holding each other.

00011110

When Ekko wakes up to take over the watch, Cyren and I are still sitting next to each other, my arm around her shoulder and her head leaning against me. I instinctively jerk away from her when I see Ekko come out of the tent, even though I'm not sure why I should feel embarrassed. When I get up and move toward the tent, I look back at Cyren. She hasn't moved from her place by the fire.

"You should get some sleep," I say.

She shrugs and says, "I'm not sure I can."

"You should try," Ekko says. "The climb up those mountains tomorrow is going to be hard."

"Maybe later."

I feel sad that the tent splits us up, but when I appear inside my own canvas-covered area, complete with a plush sleeping bag and pillow, my eyes close faster than I thought they would. My mind is running too fast for me to catch up and my thoughts become torrential, moving so fast that I can't hold onto any one of them. I'm asleep before I realize I'm lying down, but when I hear an alert for an incoming group audio-cast, it feels like I've only blinked my eyes.

I roll to one side with a groan and wave my hand in the air, opening my options screen. The corner of the screen displays the time, and I have difficulty believing I've been asleep for five hours. I glance down at the pending messages, and I see seventeen of them waiting for me. I jerk out of bed and touch the button to select the first message. Ekko's voice whispers in my ear, but I don't see any video.

"Son, I hope you're getting this. You need to wake up right now. Something is heading for our camp... and it's big."

I don't need to listen to the other messages. I push myself out of the flap, and my avatar appears in the middle of utter chaos. A bare foot the size of a truck, with coarse hair and split toenails, smashes into the ground only a few feet from where I'm standing. The entire campsite shakes and it throws me to the ground. I look up and see the bulbous belly and disfigured face of a hill giant.

I hear the rapid fire of Ekko's assault rifle erupt from the right. Bullets sink into the giant's back, only serving to annoy him. He spins just in time for Fantom to leap toward his belly. She grabs onto his belt and climbs, stabbing her sword into him repeatedly, using it as leverage to lift herself.

The hill giant wraps his chubby fingers around her body, howling in pain as he rips her from his flesh. He tosses her like she weighs nothing. I watch her body go tumbling through the air, landing over the crest of a nearby hill.

I struggle to pull my pistols from their holsters as Ekko continues to empty his magazine into the giant. The bullets manage to draw his attention, and the massive creature stomps toward the wooden avatar.

I aim both pistols at the thing's head, hoping to do more damage to his skull than the thick fat that covers the rest of him. As my explosive rounds hammer away at the scraggly hair that hangs around his face, he stops his progression toward Ekko and turns toward me. I look around and realize I have no cover, I have nowhere to run, and I'm still lying on my back.

The giant moves fast, lumbering toward me, crossing the gap with only three large steps. He reaches down and picks me up, turning his face away from my constant gunfire. His fingers squeeze my ribcage, making it hard to breathe. I keep firing, and he holds his other hand up in front of his face to block my attacks. With a quick shake that makes it feel like my head may snap from my body, my hands let go of both of my guns, leaving me helpless.

The giant smiles, revealing only three teeth inside his mouth, each one of them bigger than my head. Drool drips from the corners of his lips, and a massive tongue swirls around behind them. He draws me closer, and his mouth opens wide. I realize at that moment that I'm about to become his morning snack.

I wrestle and writhe inside his grip, trying to pry myself free, but it's impossible. Each finger is like a swollen boa constrictor, tightening itself the more I fight against it. When I get closer to his mouth, I can smell his wretched breath. Once I'm close enough to see down his rotten throat, I close my eyes. And then he rips me away from my certain doom so fast that the rush of air almost knocks me unconscious.

The giant is holding me at his side now, distracted by the incoming green fireballs that have ignited his hair. He pats his own head a few times, trying to extinguish the flames, but one hand isn't enough. He drops me to the ground as he tries to smother the green fire under his palms.

I waste no time scrambling away. My eyes are searching the ground for my pistols, but I see nothing. I keep moving. Staying alive is more important than attacking. I keep running until I'm over the top of the next hill.

As soon as I reach the top, Fantom passes me, running from the other direction. Her face looks smashed and beaten, and I see one arm hanging limp, but the look in her eyes is like a silent scream, and her clenched teeth are gnashing with hate. With her one good arm, she's holding her sword with a grip so tight it threatens to snap the blade in two. She leaps from a cluster of rocks, then activates her magical ring, striking across the sky like an arc of lightning. She smashes into the giant, her sword impaling him over and over between his eyes. The giant screams, swatting at his own face, trying to remove the attacker, but it's too late. The behemoth topples over. Fantom continues to stab his face the entire way to the ground. His back slams into the valley between the hills, crushing our campsite and sending out a concussive wave. Both arms spread out to the side and drop, lifeless. The body doesn't move, but Fantom stays on top of him, continuing to mutilate his face. Ekko climbs up next to her and joins in her battle rage, sticking the barrel of his rifle into the open mouth of the giant and unloading a series of rapid blasts.

Even splitting the awarded Koins with the group, my inventory fills with more than I'd know how to spend.

"Welcome to level 21," I hear the announcer say, then again, "Welcome to level 22."

I watch Xen climb up onto the giant's chest and set his hands on Fantom and Ekko's shoulders, saying something that finally calms them. Ekko stops firing, but the barrel of his rifle is still steaming from the constant gunfire. I stand up from my crouched position, but as I'm about to make my way down the hill to meet up with the rest of the group, I feel a hand on my back. I whirl around, my nerves still jumpy, but my breath returns to my lungs when I see Cyren's black lips forming a smile. When I look down, I see she's holding both of my pistols.

"This is becoming a habit."

"Thanks again," I say bashfully, accepting the guns and sliding them back into their holsters. "Maybe I should tie them to my hands."

"Couldn't hurt," she says with a grin.

We both walk down the hill and join the rest of the group that's standing next to the colossal body. Xen is comforting Fantom, who appears to be the most damaged. Her arm still hangs by her side, and she's trying to cover her broken face.

"Are you-" I start to ask, but realize the question is pointless when I can see for myself that she's far from okay. "Is your arm...?"

"I ain't gonna be movin' it anytime soon," she says, looking down at the useless appendage. She grabs her arm by the wrist and stuffs it into her white and yellow kimono, saying, "I'll be fine, yo. I'm only needin' one arm to swing this sword."

"Your shield," Xen says, but Fantom shrugs her one good shoulder.

"I'm sorry," Ekko says. "I tried to wake you kids up in time to run, but…"

"What were you doing still on watch?" I ask "We were supposed to take turns."

"I couldn't sleep, so I figured I'd let you get as much rest as you could."

I turn toward Cyren and ask, "Did you manage to sleep?" but she shakes her head. I let out a sigh and say, "Today is going to be rough."

"It's already been rough," Ekko says.

"I think what Arkade means is that it's going to get worse," Cyren says. "We got lucky that only one of those giants attacked us. If there had been two..." She pauses, then looks up toward the snow-capped peaks above us. "Those mountains are treacherous and built for players that are at least twenty levels higher than us. We can't fight. If we see anything, we need to run."

Everyone nods their head, but they're still reluctant.

"She's not messing around," I say to the group, then I look directly at Xen. "I don't want anyone trying to be a hero or doing anything stupid. We have one option and that's it. We go as fast as we can through this zone. Fantom leads the way to Grael with her compass."

"He's still a long way off, yo," she says, looking at her wrist. "But if we keep movin', we might be able to reach him by sundown."

Ekko loads a shell into the chamber of his gun. "Then what are we waiting for?"

00011111

In the mountainous zone, we have no choice but to stay on the trail that winds its way into the snowcapped peaks. The rest of the zone is nothing but jagged rocks and sheer cliffs covered in ice. The wind howls past us, and snow begins to fall as soon as we enter the zone, but luckily the temperature stays the same. No need for winter clothing in this game world.

The group moves slower than I want them to, and Fantom's useless arm throws off her balance. She stumbles on every slippery pathway and wobbles when we near a cliff's edge. The whole group is holding their breath, waiting for her to fall, but she never does. The pace slows to a crawl when the elevation becomes steeper, forcing us to climb up small piles of rocks. Everyone assists Fantom as best we can, but it's still a weight that we don't need.

We eventually reach a tall cliff that wraps around one side of a mountain. I can see a plateau on the other side, but we need to shimmy across a ledge that's only a few inches wide.

Fantom yells over the wind that feels stronger now that we're closer to the edge, "I'm not sure I can do this, yo."

I take a step closer to the cliff to see how far up we are and my foot slides out from under me. I catch my balance again, but I feel a sheet of ice under the thin layer of snow. There's almost no traction, and the cliff isn't offering us anything to hold on to for guidance.

"We can do this," Xen yells over the howling of the wind. "Together."

"We don't have a choice," Ekko says.

I look at the cliff, then at the group, and I say something that surprises me. "Xen's right. We need to work together." I step up toward the ledge and unfold Fantom's kimono.

"What are you doin', Cowboy?" she says, backing away.

"We're going to need your other arm for this."

"What for? It's just hangin' there, yo."

"But it's still attached." I pull out the arm, grip onto the lifeless hand, and yell back toward the group, "Everyone hold hands! If one of us slips, we have the rest of the group to stop us from falling."

Ekko shakes his head and yells up at me, "If one of us falls, they'll take the rest of us with them!"

I roll my eyes, sick of the wooden boy's constant parental concern. "I have the Anti-Gravity Belt, remember? We'll be fine."

"Why don't you cross the cliff, then throw us the belt? We can go across one at a time."

"That isn't going to work," I say with a sigh. "If you fall, you won't die, but you'll still fall. And who knows where the bottom of this cliff is. Do you want to fall down there by yourself and leave us up here without the belt?"

Nobody argues.

"Omniversalism teaches us that living together is just as important as dying together, so we should accept both with the same enthusiasm," Xen yells over the wind.

It's another of his pointless clichés that really has no bearing on logic at all. Cyren acknowledges the silliness of the statement with a smirk that tells me she finds his illogical positivity at least a bit endearing. The rest of the group reaches out and clasps their fingers around the next person's hands.

I take my first step onto the ledge, and I feel a little less than the heel of my boot resting on solid ground. My toes hang over the ledge, pointing out into the nothingness. The wind slices past my face, and I'm sure it's going to catch my trench coat like a sail and carry me off the ledge.

Inch by inch, I slide my boots sideways, never lifting them off the ledge to actually take a step. Fantom follows me, and we keep talking, letting each other know when we're going to move. She gets both feet onto the ledge, then Ekko follows her, and Xen after that. Soon all of us are looking down below, into the great emptiness of white, and only Cyren remains on the base as our anchor.

I slide my boot again, but it catches on a rough patch of ice. I jerk my leg, but it's too much. My foot slides out farther than I expect. I try to adjust, but my other leg goes out from under me. I slip, clenching Fantom's dead arm tighter. I fall slowly, but the weight of my avatar pulls her off too, and we swing under the cliff. Ekko tries to brace himself, digging his feet into the ice, but we pull him with us. Cyren manages to dig her feet into the ground and keep Xen on the ledge, but the rest of us slam into the cliff. We dangle back and forth a few times before Ekko offers his reply.

"Nice plan."

"We're alive, aren't we?"

He laughs and says, "Yeah. So now what?"

I twist myself on Fantom's arm and look up at Xen and Cyren. "How are you two doing?"

Between heavy grunts, Xen manages to say, "No problem. Take your time."

"That's sarcasm," Cyren yells down. "We can't hold you for long."

I look up at Fantom. Her face is straining as Ekko and I pull her in two different directions.

"Okay, Fantom. I need you to try to use your ring to boost our momentum when we swing."

She nods her head.

I call out directions, and the entire group works as one, swinging our line of bodies back and forth. It moves slow at first, but with every swing we pick up speed. Once we get moving, I wait until we're at the bottom of a swing, just about to curve back up, and I yell, "Now!"

Fantom's ring flashes her forward, carrying Ekko and I with her. Our bodies lift into the air, past the ledge. Xen lets go of Ekko's hand. My stomach goes up into my throat. I think it's all over, but when he lets go, our three bodies keep their momentum and we fly forward, toward the plateau on the other side of the ledge. All three of us land in the thick snow that rests there.

I'm staring into the gray sky, watching tiny flakes fall toward me, unable to speak, but I hear Xen and Cyren cheering. It doesn't take long for Cyren to be leaning over me, blocking out those falling flakes and replacing them with her black-lipped smile.

"I'm going to be honest with you," she says. "I'm kind of surprised that worked."

I hear Ekko say, "I think all of us are."

"All that matters right now is that it did," Xen says. "Omniversalism teaches us that what might happen tomorrow is more important than what could have happened yesterday."

I lift myself out of the snow and climb to my feet. The flakes increase in density, and I'm having a hard time seeing the rest of the group, even though they're only a few feet away.

"We should keep moving," I say. "This snow will give us cover. We should take advantage while it lasts."

"It will also make it harder for us to see the NPCs," Cyren says.

"She's right," Ekko says. "We could walk right into the middle of a group of... of whatever, and we wouldn't even know until we were right on top of them."

"There ain't no time to argue, yo," Fantom calls out from the deep white. Her voice sounds far away. "I'm leavin'. You comin' with me or not?"

I hear footsteps as people jog to catch up to her. I smile. Her brute logic cuts through the nonsense. She reminds them all that we don't have time to stand around and debate. We need to act. Left or right. Up or down. We need to go with our gut and deal with the consequences.

We all walk close together so that we won't lose anyone. We're barely able to see each other through the growing blizzard. As the wind increases and the flakes blow horizontally, I feel Cyren's fingers wrap around my own. I look toward her. I can't see her face, but I know she's there, and it makes me feel safer. She makes me feel protected. She makes me feel like I'm a part of something. For the first time, it's something I *want* to be a part of. She gives my hand a little squeeze, and right then I decide that I never want to play solo again.

00100000

We're all lying on our bellies, looking down at a military base built into the side of the mountain. The only road travels straight through the cement walls with tall, reinforced gates blocking either side. Armed guards patrol the road in front of both gates, and when I zoom in with my goggles, I can see men with rifles in the towers that sit on either side of the gates. The place appears impenetrable and far beyond our level.

"This doesn't look good," Ekko says, his wooden image fluttering in and out of focus.

"There's gotta be another way." Fantom's voice doesn't sound as sure as her words.

I scan around the mountain with my goggles, zooming in and out of the terrain. The fortress rests on a ledge, with the walls bordering both sides. A cliff rises up on one side of the base and drops off on the other. There's no way around the structure.

"We have to go through."

"That's suicide," Ekko says. "The sheer number of soldiers down there will tear us apart."

"We can't go in, guns blazin'," Fantom says. "But maybe if we use stealth…"

"You're both right," Cyren says. "These soldiers are programmed to overwhelm us with their numbers because individually they're low level NPCs. We can't possibly take on the whole base, but look at them. They aren't always in groups. If we can take them out one at a time, without alerting the others..."

"You and Fantom are our best bet," I say. "Your attacks are silent. The rest of us are going to be nearly useless." I grit my teeth with regret. "I should have bought those silencers for my pistols."

Fantom looks toward Cyren and says, "Boys, yo. They're never plannin' ahead."

Cyren doesn't get the joke, or maybe she just ignores it. She points at the front gate and says, "When the sun goes down, I'll take out the men on the ground. You can use your ring to get up into those towers."

Fantom nods and says, "Sounds good, yo. Once we take 'em out, move down to the gate. If things go bad, we'll open those doors so you can give us some backup."

"If things go bad," Ekko says, "we're all dead."

I slap the wooden boy's shoulder and say, "Then we've got nothing to lose."

We lie perfectly still for the rest of the afternoon, watching the sun creep down into the east. The view is spectacular from where we are, with the lights of the city blinking to life in the fading sunshine. When the sun completely disappears, and the towers turn on their spotlights, Cyren and Fantom decide to make their move.

As they stand up to leave, I grab Cyren's hand and say, "Be careful."

She shakes her head at me. "It's too dangerous down there for me to be careful." Then she smiles. "But I promise I'll be precise."

With the combination of the falling snow and the darkness of night, Ekko and Xen can hardly see anything. I use my goggles and try to give them play-by-plays as the action unfolds, but most of it happens too fast.

I watch Cyren and Fantom skirt down opposite sides of the hill, sliding on the snow to make their advance as low and quick as possible. They dodge the spotlights easily, the pattern simple and obvious. Snowbanks hide their slow advancement to the wall, and when they reach the soldiers, they waste no time attacking.

Cyren leaps out from behind a mound of snow, her arms outstretched, flinging white flakes to the sides like wings. She lands on the back of one guard, bounces off him, and spin-kicks the other guard in the face. When the third guard raises his gun at her, I think that their stealth attack is going to fail before they've had a chance to begin. Cyren scoops up a handful of snow, tossing it at him as a distraction. By the time the snow has fallen away from his face, her fist is crushing his nose. She does a back flip and finishes off the first two guards. The whole thing looks like a well-choreographed gymnastics routine.

I lift my gaze to the towers, but Fantom is already dispatching one of the guards. She slices his rifle in half, then cuts him in two at the waist. His body splits and drops to the floor. She leaps from the tower and uses her ring to flash across the air, landing safely on the other tower. Her wide-bladed sword arcs through the air and lops off the other rifleman's head. She does this all with one arm.

I look back down at Cyren. She's already scaling the wall, climbing up to where Fantom is waiting for her.

"They're going over the wall, so I won't be able to see them anymore," I explain to Xen and Ekko.

I hear Fantoms's voice in my ear. "Not true, yo."

A screen appears in front of me and I see a video-cast from her viewpoint.

"How are you—"

"It's just like Xen's audio-cast," she says. "That's what gave me the idea."

We all lean forward, drawn into the first-person perspective of the camera. The quality of the feed is crystal clear, and I forget I'm not actually down there with them.

Fantom looks over the edge of the tower, down into the heart of the facility. Soldiers wander from building to building, but they use the wide open courtyard to store vehicles. We see tanks and armored personnel carriers, but as she scans the entire base, we all see the one thing that Xen has been wanting since the first time he laid eyes on it. Parked in the middle of the courtyard is some kind of advanced airplane, with wings that turn upright to allow for vertical takeoff, armed with eight missiles and two huge rotary cannons.

"The jet!" he says, almost shouting with excitement.

He slaps his own hand over his own mouth so that I don't have to keep him quiet. I still give him a stern look, and he apologizes with his eyes.

We look back at the video-cast and watch the two girls slide down the tower wall, quickly making their way across the open courtyard and hiding behind one of the parked tanks. A guard comes wandering around the corner of the vehicles, and Cyren slaps her hands onto either side of his head. With a twist, his head spins, his neck cracks, and his body drops to the ground.

Fantom points to the open courtyard, and Cyren nods at her. She takes off running, bolting from vehicle to vehicle, stopping only to make sure no one is watching before making her next move. Fantom turns her attention to the main building, which looks to be only two stories tall, but has a huge communications array on the roof. She sneaks along the wall, outside of the main lights of the facility and past a small bunker. As she's passing the bunker, she peeks into one of the windows and sees a room full of sleeping soldiers, all of them lying on bunk beds.

"Apparently even NPCs gotta sleep," she whispers.

She turns her attention back to the main building. She looks around the corner to watch the soldiers that are coming and going from the door. She's smart. I hear her whispering to herself as she counts the seconds between each soldier.

After a few seconds she sighs and whispers, "I ain't sure I got the time to find the pattern." There's a pause. "Whatever," she says as the next soldier exits the doorway, and she leaps out from the corner.

The soldier reaches for the pistol on his side, but Fantom swipes her sword and cuts his hand off at the wrist. He opens his mouth to scream just as her sword swings around, and his head rolls off from his body.

"Hide the body! The other guards might come across it," Xen shouts at the screen.

"I ain't gotta," Fantom says, looking out into the courtyard. "Cyren's takin' care of them, yo."

Her video-cast only gives us a glimpse, but one by one, each guard roaming around outside disappears into the shadows, dispatched in the blackness by a leather-strapped fist.

00100001

Fantom opens the door of the main building just enough to peek through the opening. A soldier is standing a few feet from her, turning a dial on the wall. As she steps in the doorway, I'm about to tell her to wait, but it's too late. Her sword stabs through his neck, preventing him from making any kind of noise, but then she turns to look to her right, toward the direction that she couldn't see through the open door. Four guards stand in the hall looking straight at her, slack-jawed. She reacts before they do, throwing the wide blade of her sword down the hall. It sinks into the chest of one of the guards, throwing him onto his back. As the other three guards step back, their eyes bulging at the sight of the sword sticking out of the body, they all reach for the rifles slung over their shoulders.

Fantom races down the hall, stomping her foot onto the stabbed guard for leverage as she yanks the blade out of his body. The hallway is small and the three guards have a hard time maneuvering around each other. Fantom uses this to her advantage, stabbing her sword low, cutting two of the guards off at the knees. They topple over, but one of them manages to squeeze the trigger of his rifle. The gun lets out a burst of loud shots that echo through the hallway. Fantom grabs a hold of the barrel and pushes it toward the third guard, filling him with bullets. Two more stabs and the legless guards stop moving.

"We got a problem, yo," Fantom says as she races for the stairway at the end of the hall.

"I heard the gunfire," Cyren says, "and so did the rest of the base."

Xen, Ekko, and I are already on our feet, running as fast as we can through the deep snow, sliding most of the way down the hill toward the front gate. As we near the wall, the doors begin to open, and Cyren is standing on the other side.

Xen's hands are already on fire, and he's tossing the green balls of flame at the guards coming out of the buildings. They look disoriented, their eyes scanning the empty courtyard for signs of the attack. The explosion of fire from Xen's magic engulfs huge groups of them. I give him a quick glance of surprise, wondering how much he managed to level from the hill giant's death.

Ekko fires, covering me as I run with Cyren, trying to close the gap between us and the guards, but by the time I reach a shooting distance, the NPCs are already firing back. Bullets spray around me, and I hear rounds flying past my head, inches from my ears. I spin behind an armored personnel carrier and their rounds bounce harmlessly off the metal shell.

Cyren dives into the ground, rolling underneath a tank and out the other side. She ducks behind another vehicle to keep her attackers guessing.

Ekko sprays another burst of fire at the growing amount of guards, then steps into the doorway of the tower. I see his feet disappear up the ladder as he moves himself into a better position.

Xen steps out from behind a tank, a wave of fire pouring from his palms like a flamethrower, igniting a group of soldiers who are too busy firing on my position to see him flank them from the other side.

When I hear the gunfire stop, I spin around from the corner of the vehicle and let explosive rounds fly from both pistols. I blast apart five soldiers, blowing their NPC avatars to pieces before the other soldiers return fire. A few shells strike me in the chest, a few more in my arm, but I spin back around the vehicle.

I glance at the screen displaying Fantom's video-cast, which is still open in the corner of my view. Muzzle flares and rapid movements make it hard to see what's happening, but she seems to be in some kind of control room. Monitor screens line the walls and the men she's cutting down are wearing officer's uniforms.

I peek around the vehicle when Ekko fires from the top of the tower. The burst of automatic fire from his raised position drops a handful of soldiers and scatters the rest. I step out and fire again, hitting a few of the stragglers that aren't as quick to reach cover. I watch Cyren make her way around one of the buildings, and seconds later I see bodies fly out from behind the wall, landing on their backs, unconscious.

I spin behind the vehicle and smile. I think we might actually manage to pull off our plan. Fantom and Cyren took out quite a few of the NPCs before they were alerted to our presence, and now we're striking from different positions, spreading out the mass of soldiers so they can't overwhelm us. Our team is well balanced, with smart enough players, and if we stay focused, we might actually get through this mess.

I glance down at the video-cast from Fantom, and I watch her drive her sword into the last officer. She scans around the room. The disrupted graphics on the computer displays roll over themselves, and sparks fly from damaged electronics. Bodies lie over desks and in piles on the floor. When she doesn't see any more attackers, she walks to the window and looks out over the courtyard to see how we're doing. The high-definition image affords me a strange bird's eye view, but then I see something in the glass. A reflection. Movement. Fantom doesn't notice it. I use the screen's controls to zoom in on the image and see one of the officers crawl up from the floor, his arm barely reaching a set of controls.

I scream into the camera, "Turn around!"

Fantom spins in time to see the dying NPC flip open a plastic box on the desk and slam his palm down on a large red button underneath it.

I hear the sound blasting from both the video-cast screen, and the courtyard. A horn shakes the ground like a force of nature, blowing an alarm that could wake a god. The noise stuns everyone, including the soldiers. Most of them stop firing their weapons and look into the sky. The sound echoes against the cliff walls, shaking rocks and snow loose from the top of the mountain. Boulders come crashing down, slamming into the vehicles and buildings, rolling across the courtyard, flattening soldiers underneath their crushing weight.

When the sound stops, I look back at the screen and see Fantom removing her sword from the officer who pushed the button. She looks down at the controls, but there are no labels or markings whatsoever.

"What was that?" she asks, but before I can say anything in reply, the horn blasts again.

I cover my ears, the noise causing my eardrums to swell. I peek around the armored vehicle again, and I see the NPC soldiers dropping their weapons. They fall to their knees, some of them screaming, others whimpering. Their programming stuns me. It's like they aren't concerned with us anymore. I notice many of them searching the sky, like they're looking for something. That's when I notice the insignia painted on the side of the vehicle for the first time.

It's a symbol of a red dragon.

00100010

The horn blows five times. When it stops, the silence is unsettling. The soldiers in the courtyard stay on their knees, pressing their faces into the ground with their arms outstretched like they're all in the midst of a group prayer. Ekko stays in the tower, keeping his gun trained on the soldiers, but Cyren and Xen come out from their hiding spot, walking among the NPCs and holding up their hands to each other to express their confusion. I'm about to warn them what I think is going to happen, but unfortunately, there's no need.

The sound of massive wings flapping in the air overwhelms the howl of the frigid mountain air. It sounds like the canvas of a ship catching a gust of wind, mixed with thunder rolling through clouds from. I look into the air, waiting for the giant creature to come swooping down like an incarnation of death itself, snatching me from the game world, but I don't see anything. Only snow falls from the black sky. The sound of the wings ricochets off the walls of the base, making it seem to come from every direction.

I look over at Xen and Cyren. They're both spinning around, still unsure of what they're hearing. I open my mouth and scream with all the power in my lungs.

"*Drrraaagon!*"

As if I was announcing its arrival, the beast rises up from the cliffs below, its wingspan spreading out so far in each direction that it could envelop the entire mountain. Its clawed feet grab onto the walls of the military base, cracking the concrete as if it was brittle sand. The muscles that make up its torso look like thick, scale-covered ropes, intertwined and coiling around themselves, flexing with even the slightest movement. Its long neck reels back, holding its horned head high above us, its bulbous eyes searching the area below for prey.

The soldiers keep their faces pressed against the ground, but Cyren and Xen stand in the middle of them, looking straight up at the giant creature lording over the cliff side, too stunned to move. I see the dragon's eyes spot them, its pupils shrinking as it sees the only two people who are standing upright. I watch its head go back. Its throat inflates, growing like a round balloon. I've seen enough fantasy video-casts to know what's coming next.

Luckily, so does Cyren. She grabs Xen's arm and runs. They weave through the cluster of praying soldiers, reaching the side of a building just as the dragon opens its mouth. Liquid fire pours from between its teeth like burning vomit. The flames disintegrate the soldiers caught in the flood, their avatars melting with the snow.

I realize when the dragon inhales, readying itself for another attack, that I'm just standing there, watching the carnage. My feet haven't moved since the dragon appeared. I haven't blinked. I haven't breathed. I suck in air and hear Ekko screaming in my ear.

"Do I take the shot? Someone tell me what to do!"

"Don't do it, yo," Fantom says. "Your gun ain't gonna do any damage. Not at your level."

"So what's the plan? Sit back and wait to die?"

The dragon lets loose another blast, this time puking its fire onto the opposite side of the building where Cyren and Xen chose to hide. The roof and walls dissolve into the ground, revealing the interior like someone cut the building in half. Cyren and Xen run toward me, dodging behind the armored personnel carriers. Their eyes are expectant, wanting an answer when they reach me, and yet I still haven't moved. When I see Cyren's face inches away from mine, the panic in her eyes shatters my frozen state of shock.

I turn away from her and scan my surroundings, soaking in the entire battlefield in one deep breath. I push past the chaos and add up the entire equation. I see melted avatars. I see burning buildings. I see crushed armored personnel carriers. And I see tanks. I turn back to my group members, grab Xen by the shoulders, and point across the courtyard.

"I need you to lay down cover. I need the biggest wall of flames you can raise."

Xen nods his head. His hands burst with fire, and he steps out from behind the vehicle. He stretches out his arms high in the air, and a line of flames grow from the ground. The dragon turns toward him, but the green fire hypnotizes the beast for a moment.

The flames grow quickly, and when they're nearly twenty feet high, I grab Cyren's wrist and run. But there's no need to drag her behind me. She runs at my side. Our feet dig into the ground with every step, pushing us farther, faster. When we reach the tanks, we split with only a slight glance into each other's eyes. She leaps to the hatch on the top of her tank with one jump, but I need to climb up the side like everyone else.

I take a look back at Xen right before I drop inside, and I see him backing away as the dragon leans its head down close to the flames. The creature takes a deep breath and inhales the entire wall of fire, extinguishing it instantly. Xen runs for the front gate, hoping to hide outside the walls of the fortress, but I don't have time to make sure he gets there before the dragon exhales.

I fall into a seat, looking at the mess of instruments in front of me. I ignore the directions written in the middle of the panel explaining to players how to drive the vehicle. I don't need to move. I'm only interested in one thing this tank can do. I spot a visor hanging from the ceiling with wires and tubes protruding from it, but more importantly, I see a trigger.

That I know how to use.

I push my face into the visor, and I see an electronic display of the courtyard in front of me with a cross-hair in the middle of the screen. I spin the reticle to my right, pointing it up at the dragon that's spitting fire again, this time melting the front gate. I swallow hard, assuming its flames can eat through the shell of the tank as well.

I center the cross-hair on the dragon's chest and pull the trigger, but nothing happens. I see a warning appear on the screen, letting me know that there's no round in the chamber. I look to my right and see a line of the giant shells sitting in boxes on the floor. An open slot sits above them. I grab a shell that's three times the size of a brick and set it into the open door. It fits perfectly, and with a shove, the doorway slides shut.

I look in the visor again and see the dragon inhaling, readying itself to destroy even more of the mountain fortress. I center the cross-hair and pull the trigger. The cannon fires with a deep explosion, rattling the entire tank and vibrating the teeth in my mouth. The shell blasts into the dragon's hide, and I see scales go flying. The creature lets loose a high-pitched screech into the air and almost falls off the wall, but with a few flaps of its wings, it pulls itself upright and narrows its eyes at me.

I reach down, my heart racing as I drop another shell into the chamber. I slide the door shut and grab the visor with both hands. The dragon's throat has already swelled, ready to let loose another load of burning bile, just as Cyren's cannon fires. Her shell slams into the inflated throat, and the balloon-like larynx pops open.

Liquid fire pours from the opening like molten lava. The dragon flails around, its wings flapping wildly as it uselessly claws at its own wound. It topples off the wall, falling over the cliff. For a brief moment, I actually believe we've won, but the dragon comes swooping back over the wall, its throat still hanging open, raw and exposed. I unload another shell, but it flies to the left, and the round harmlessly shoots off into the distance.

The dragon's head looks at both of us, back and forth, deciding which to attack. I dive for the shells, loading another into the chamber. When I look back into the visor, the dragon is still floating above us, but I can see his eyes locked on Cyren's tank. Without the ability to breath fire, the dragon resorts to a more brutal attack. It swoops down, landing right next to us, impacting the ground like a small bomb and shaking the tank. I unload another round, but it barely notices the annoying projectile slam into its shoulder. The dragon lifts its clawed paw and swipes at Cyren's tank, throwing the vehicle across the courtyard like a child's toy before she gets off another shot. The tank rolls over and over, eventually crashing against the far wall.

I see the dragon turn its attention toward me, and I pull myself away from the visor, trying to load yet another round into the chamber. Just when I'm about to drop the shell into the doorway, the tank rolls. Up becomes down, and my body is slamming against every side of the interior. The boxes of shells spill everywhere, and my world continues to spin. My arms bend in unnatural positions, and when the tank stops rolling, the weight of a computer display torn from the wall pins my legs to the floor.

00100011

I lift my left arm, pain striking through my shoulder and into my neck, but I manage to gesture in the air and open Fantom's video-cast screen. She's hiding in the control room, searching the video screens for something, anything to use against the dragon.

Ekko is screaming in my ear, "Is everyone okay? Is anyone still alive? Talk to me. Someone. Please."

I feel some kind of relief when I hear Cyren's voice say, "I'm here. But my tank is upside down, and I can't get the turret to move. I won't be able to fire again."

I grunt, trying to speak, but I only manage to say, "I... can't."

There's a pause, and it lingers. The silence in the group voice communication goes on for far too long, and I suspect no one knows what to do. I have a feeling anyone still able to move is considering how far they could get if they just ran away. I know it's what I'd be thinking.

Then I hear Xen's voice. Of course it's Xen's voice. "There's one vehicle left… and it's all mine."

Fantom and Ekko are yelling at him. They're telling him to stay hidden. They're telling him that he'll never make it. They're telling him that it's suicide to even try. But I don't waste my breath. Xen isn't going to listen.

Fantom runs to the window of the control center and looks down on the courtyard. Through her video-cast, I can see the tiny monk in the orange wrappings running as fast as he can to the small landing pad of the fighter jet. The dragon sees him and stomps his feet toward what must look to the creature like an insignificant bug. I watch Xen scurry through burning pits of fire in the decimated landscape, moving his legs as fast as they'll go, but it's not enough.

I feel detached. The screen makes it all feel unreal, like it isn't actually happening just outside of the tank.

The dragon gets closer and leans back on its hind legs, ready to pounce forward and squash the little man with one clawed foot. It stretches out its paw, the sharp talons gleaming in the firelight, when a small explosion ignites on its back. The dragon turns, annoyed, and another explosion hits its chest. Fantom searches for the source of the attack and finally turns her view toward the lookout tower where Ekko positioned himself. The wooden boy launches another grenade, this time striking the dragon in the side of its head. It doesn't do any damage, but it's enough to annoy the beast. It lets out a roar of anger and moves toward Ekko, ignoring Xen's seemingly pointless race across the courtyard.

"Ekko! What are you doin'?" Fantom yells into the group voice-cast. "It's comin' right for you, yo!"

"I see that," he grunts.

The wooden boy backs away from the dragon, pressing himself against the far wall of the box on top of the tower. I can see him looking over the side, wondering if he could survive the jump, but his hesitation takes too long. The dragon spins its entire body, lashing its elongated tail at the tower. The huge appendage smashes into the concrete with a thick wallop, crumbling the stone structure into a cloud of debris. The spotlight explodes, sending sparks and glass spraying in every direction. I close my eyes, waiting to hear the game announce Ekko's death.

But nothing comes.

I open one eye, then the other, and as the concrete dust fades in the wind, I see the flickering image of Ekko floating in midair, as if he were still crouched down inside the top of the lookout tower. He keeps flickering, then shifts to the side, then back again, stuck in some kind of bandwidth lag.

The game didn't register the strike against him.

When his connection catches back up with the world, his solid image drops onto the crumbled tower only a few feet below him.

"You lucky—"

Fantom cuts me off, yelling, "He made it, yo!" as the view of the video-cast spins back toward Xen, who's now lowering the canopy over the cockpit of the jet.

The dragon returns his attention to the tiny monk, but as it stomps its way back across the fortress, Xen already has the engine started and is lifting off from the ground.

I hear him repeating, "Oh wow, oh wow, oh wow," as the plane lifts high above the ledge, out of the dragon's reach.

The creature tries to swipe at the jet, standing tall on its hind legs, but as soon as the dragon reaches into the air, Xen turns the engines forward and pierces the clouds like a rocket-powered arrowhead. The dragon roars and flaps its wings faster, pushing itself higher into the air. It dives off the cliff to pick up speed and swoops back up, chasing after Xen.

Another screen opens next to Fantom's video-cast, this one showing the inside of a cockpit.

"I can't believe this," Xen says. "I'm flying!"

His voice is shaking. His adrenalin is fueling every movement. He pushes forward on the stick and the jet dives back toward the mountains. He pulls back and does a barrel roll, spinning into the air. Drumbeats pound in my ears, accompanied by an electric guitar and a woman's screeching vocals. I cringe when I realize he's chosen a soundtrack.

I yell at the screen, "Xen! You need to take this seriously. You might be our only hope of taking this thing down."

"I know!" He turns down the volume on the music and says more calmly, "I've... I've got this. Trust me." The jet banks to the right and curves back around toward us. "As soon as I find the dragon, that is."

"You gotta use your radar, yo."

I watch his video-cast viewpoint tilt down as he looks at the wall of controls wrapping around him. In the center is a small green circle with a line spinning around it. As the line passes the bottom of the circle, a small blip appears.

"There," I yell at the screen, "it's behind you."

Xen turns in his seat and looks out the back of the glass canopy that surrounds the cockpit. The red body of the dragon bursts out of a cloud behind the jet.

"Son, you need to keep your speed up," Ekko says. "It doesn't have its fire breath anymore, so it'll need to attack you with its claws—"

"Or tail," Fantom interjects.

"Right," Ekko continues. "If you can keep the jet away from—"

A scraping noise cuts Ekko off, and the jet wobbles in the air. Xen turns around again and sees long claw marks down one of the wings. He looks down at the throttle on his side and pushes it forward. The whine of the engines grow and the clouds whip past him even faster.

"He needs to get that dragon in front of him," I say, "where he can actually use his weapons."

"It's going to be hard," Cyren adds. "The dragon can't match his speed, but it makes up for that with its maneuverability."

Xen banks to the left and does a barrel roll. He yanks back on the control stick, pulling the nose up until the jet is flying upside down. He keeps pulling back until the plane has flipped around and is pointing downward. The dragon tries to follow him, but it can't pick up the same kind of speed as it climbs into the air. It stops and turns toward the jet, but now Xen is aiming right at the giant beast.

"How was that?" Xen asks.

"Fire your guns!" Ekko yells.

The dual rotary cannons mounted on the nose of the jet spit out tracer rounds, each one lighting up as they spray across the sky. The dragon flails in mid-air as each bullet strikes its body, tearing another hole into its thick hide. Holes open in its giant wings, and the dragon flops in the sky, barely able to keep itself afloat. Xen flies straight at the beast, unloading both cannons, turning the barrels white hot as they throw death at the monster. He gets closer and closer until I realize he isn't going to turn.

Ekko beats me to it, screaming, "Don't get so close to—"

It's too late. As Xen closes in on the dragon, it turns to the side and tears its claws into one of the wings. Xen spins, rolls through the sky, and then yanks on the stick, forcing the plane to right itself. It still wavers, but he gains control back over the machine.

"Wow," he says. "That was close."

00100100

"You need to keep your distance," I say. "Use your missiles. They should be able to lock on to the dragon's heat signature."

"And you damaged its wings, yo," Fantom says. "That should make it easier to outmaneuver."

Xen looks down at his radar and banks the jet, turning around to make another run at the dragon. When he gets the small blip in front of him, he looks out his canopy and sees the dragon try to lift itself higher into the air. It's struggling, stretching its neck out as far as it can.

Xen pushes the stick forward and dives, but when he gets closer to the dragon, he pulls back up, coming at the beast from below, where it isn't looking. He flips open a switch on his control stick and activates his missiles. A targeting display appears on the glass of the canopy, and Xen adjusts his climb so that the tiny square matches up with his cross-hair. When they do, both icons turn red, and he hears a beeping noise.

"Say a prayer for our fire-breathing friend."

Two missiles fire from each wing, spiraling through the air, straight at the dragon. It doesn't see them coming, and when they hit, they cause an explosion much bigger than I was expecting. Boiling flames and rolling smoke erupt in a giant ball of heat, the concussive blast shaking the jet. Xen continues toward the detonation, waiting to see how much damage he has done. As he climbs closer to the black smoke, it begins to fade, and he sees the dragon's body, blown apart and falling in pieces. A leg falls in one direction, and an arm falls in another, but the main body comes streaming out of the smoke straight at the jet.

He pulls back on the throttle and yanks the control stick to the right, but the dragon's eyes open wide, and it reaches out for the jet with the only arm that's still attached. Its frayed wings furiously wave in the air, pushing it toward Xen. For a second I think he's banking enough to get out of the way, but at the last moment the dragon pushes forward and manages to wrap its claws around the nose of the cockpit. This gives it something to pull on, and it yanks its broken body closer, allowing it to sink its teeth into the already damaged wing. The weight of the dragon pulls the plane down, pointing the nose of the aircraft straight toward DangerWar City.

The dragon's tail curls up and pierces through one of the engines. It yanks the tip of the appendage free, then jams it into the plane again, this time breaking into the cockpit. The huge pointed tail bursts right through the controls and slices off one of Xen's legs.

"Eject!" Fantom yells. "Eject!"

Xen grabs the yellow lever next to his seat and yanks on it, but the lever breaks free from the console, damaged by the dragon's tail. He remains sealed inside the cockpit, rushing toward the ground.

The entire group is screaming, but I can't hear them over my own voice. I'm yelling something, but it's unintelligible. I'm babbling nonsense and barely forming words. I can see Xen's death approaching, and there's nothing I can do about it. I lie there, on the floor of the tank, watching it all happen in the small screen of his video-cast.

The buildings grow in size. Xen stops wrestling with the control stick, and gives up trying to make it react to his movements. When the plane roars past the top of a skyscraper, he unloads the rest of his missiles. All six of them fire from his wings, but at the speed he's going, they race right next to him, straight toward the street. I realize he's trying to cause the biggest explosion he can. If he's going to die, he's going to make sure that dragon dies with him.

As the street gets so close that I can see the details of the cars, I hear Xen say something, and though his voice is moderate and calm, I can still hear it clearly over the burst of the jet engines, the roar of the dragon clinging to his plane, and the screams of my group members.

"Don't worry, Kade. I'm just happy we got to play together."

And then the screen of his video-cast turns to static.

I hear the explosion in the distance. It sounds faint, just a low rumble. Fantom's video-cast is at the southern window of the control tower, looking out toward the city. A skyscraper is toppling over, and a pillar of smoke is growing into the sky.

I close the video-cast and turn off the group audio-cast. There's nothing I could say, even if I wanted to communicate. There's nothing anyone could say. I don't want to hear anyone's voice. I want silence, but all I hear is the constant ringing of a seeming endless supply of Koins dumping into my inventory. I can barely hear the announcer's voice over the sound effect.

"Group member Xen has died."

I don't cry. I can't even breathe. The emptiness I feel inside my chest doesn't allow it. I close my eyes and try to put myself somewhere else. I want to be anywhere else. At that moment, I'd even take the real world over where I am. I wish there was another virtual world inside this one. I wish I could go even deeper inside myself, some place that no one else could go. Some place where no one could touch me. Some place where no one could hurt me.

I hear the announcer say, "Congratulations, you have killed the Great Demon of the Darkfyre Mountains," but I couldn't care less.

I didn't kill anything but my friend.

So when he says, "Welcome to level 23. Welcome to level 24. Welcome to level 25. Welcome to level 26. Welcome to level 27. Welcome to level 28," and doesn't stop until I finally hear, "Welcome to level 49," I get no pleasure from my sudden rise in power.

I lie in the tank for what feels like hours, but the game clock tells me it's a little under ten minutes. I never turn the group audiocast back on, so when the hatch above me opens, it's surprising. I look up into the light shining through the hole and see Cyren's face peering down at me. She looks worried, forcing an encouraging smile toward me. She climbs inside and lifts the computer console off my legs.

"You should have chosen strength," she says lightheartedly, but I don't reply. She looks at me, her eyes shaking in their sockets, and says, "I'm sorry, Arkade." She looks away and says again, "I'm *so*, so sorry."

She helps me to my feet, exerting most of the effort to get me upright. Surprisingly, my legs don't hurt. I'm able to climb out of the tank without much strain, though it takes mental effort that I'm not sure I possess anymore. When I get outside, the fortress around me looks decimated. Walls are crumbling, fires still burn, and the bodies of NPC avatars lie around us like debris. Fantom and Ekko are staring up at me, waiting for some kind of reaction, but I give none. I am stone.

Ekko speaks first, trying to push past the obvious topic and get straight to the point.

"We need rest. We should—"

"No," I say, cutting off his suggestion. "I want to get this over with. I want to find this Grael, and I want to figure out a way to save Xen."

"Do you think you can still save him?" Ekko asks, and I see Fantom slap his arm. "What? I'm just asking. How do we know—"

"Because I know," I say with a stern tone, speaking through my clenched jaw.

Ekko opens his mouth to say something, but I'm already walking away, toward the other gate. I pass the bodies of the NPCs, but I can't look at them. Even though they're only part of the game, they look too real. They just make me think of Xen's avatar. And then I realize his avatar doesn't even exist. The explosion would have disintegrated him. Xen isn't in the game world, or the real world. He's somewhere in between.

My knees give out on me. I fall into the snow, and my body folds in half. I start to shake, and I realize that in my E-Womb, in the real world, my body is crying. I don't hold back. I let loose, weeping into the snow.

Cyren is at my side in seconds. She lifts me out of the white powder and wraps her arms around me. She holds me close, saying nothing. There's nothing to say, and I'm happy that she isn't disrespectful enough to pretend that there is. She's just there, letting me rest my head on her shoulder. She covers me with her embrace, protecting me from any more harm.

When my body empties itself of every last tear, I lie calmly against her. She takes off my hat and runs her fingers across my scalp, brushing the stray hairs that are stuck to my face. I feel safe. I want to stay there forever.

I feel a hand on my back, and I look up toward Fantom. She's touching me, saying nothing, but offering me her support. Ekko does the same. Our bodies all shudder under his lag, vibrating and flickering in and out of a solid connection. I close my eyes, and I feel the group as one entity. No matter the pain I might be feeling, I also feel like I'm a part of something other than myself, and that feels good.

00100101

We follow the road higher into the mountains for another ten kilometers. I hold Cyren's hand the entire walk. I'm unwilling to let go. I need to know she's there, and I need her to know I'm there too.

The snow becomes deeper and the wind becomes stronger the higher into the mountains we get, but the world around us feels empty. No traps lie in wait, no NPCs leap out to attack, and other than the environmental sound effects of creatures off in the distance, the zone is barren.

When we reach yet another curve in the road, Fantom stops us. I've been noticing her rubbing her stomach, and a few times her steps have been less than straight. She's feeling the pangs of hunger, but she won't admit it. She brushes the snow off the compass on her wrist and points toward a small winding trail that leads into a cluster of trees.

"He's this way, yo."

No one says anything more. We follow her silently into the forest. The trees give us a small relief from the wind and snow, creating a natural canopy around us, but it also blocks out the small amount of light that was reflecting from the moon. Ekko turns on the flashlight mounted on the end of his rifle, but it doesn't offer much light. I can't help thinking that Xen could summon his green flames to light our way. I have to catch my breath and block that thought from destroying me.

The trail continues to wind its way through the forest, the elevation increasing with every step until the rocks that we're walking on become crudely carved stairs. At the top of the climb, we find a cave entrance covered in cobwebs. Ekko shines his flashlight through the webs, but we can't see much in the endless darkness. None of us know what to expect, so we step slowly through the mouth of the cavern. We examine the walls and ceiling before going any deeper. We all expect something to jump out at us.

"The compass is pointin' deeper into the cave."

"Just be careful," Ekko says, his wooden body shaking with lag. "We don't know what kind of quest they designed this cave to contain. There could be traps, or magic, or... anything."

Fantom nods and says, "I'm feelin' a little better knowin' that we're not so far below the intended level for this zone."

"Thanks to Xen," I say.

No one says anything else.

The cavern curves its way deeper into the mountain, twisting left and right like the body of a snake. The flashlight flickers off the wall, casting moving shadows that make us all jumpy. The tunnel eventually opens into a large cavernous area, with water pooling far below a thin bridge made of stone. On the other side of the bridge is another cave entrance, but a flat circular stone covers the opening.

"We're close," Fantom says, and steps out onto the bridge.

The stone creaks under her weight. There's no need to put more strain on the thin rock, so Ekko doesn't follow until after Fantom has completely traversed to the other side. Cyren goes next, and I follow her. I'm only halfway across when a chunk of the bridge breaks under my foot. I hear the group scream as the entire bridge starts to crumble. My Anti-Gravity Belt gives me the extra second I need to run to the other side of the bridge before the entire thing turns to small pieces of stone and drops into the water below us. Cyren gives me a hug once I'm safe.

Fantom looks at her compass and points toward the circular stone. "He's on the other side of this, yo."

"He's a magic user," I say. "His element is earth."

Ekko looks around the giant cavern and asks, "Is he actually powerful enough to have created all this himself?"

I shrug, but I'm starting to think it's possible.

Ekko stands on one side of the flat, circular stone and tries to roll it to the side. It doesn't budge at all, almost as if someone has secured it to the wall.

"Explosives?" Fantom asks.

"I wouldn't dare use them in an underground cavern," Ekko says, "Who knows what kind of cave-in feature they programmed into this thing."

I ask Cyren, "Care to test that strength attribute?"

She humbly nods her head and steps up to the doors. She digs her feet into the ground and pulls a fist back behind her waist. With a sudden exhale, she punches the rock, blowing huge pieces through the other side. The entire circular stone crumbles apart, falling to the side and tumbling into the water.

Ekko chuckles and says, "Yeah, well, I probably loosened it for you."

We all step through the doorway into a large, circular room. It looks carved like the tunnel and cavern behind us, but the walls appear smoother, as if someone spent more time working on it than the rest. A pool of water sits against one wall, and in the middle of the room is an activated camping item.

"He must be here," Cyren says.

As soon as the final word exits her mouth, I see her drop out of the corner of my eye. The wall behind her changes, turning from solid rock into a soft pudding. It reaches out like an amorphous blob, consuming her entire body and pulling her back toward the wall. I reach out to grab her, but she's ripped from me. The wall completely traps her body when the stone solidifies again, locking her into place. Only her head remains free.

I hear a rustling from the corner of the room, and I see the player named Grael step out from the shadows. His avatar looks the same as when he first attacked me. Camouflage pants, bullet-proof vest, tattooed arms, red dreadlocks tied behind his head, and that old gas mask strapped to his face. He walks toward us confidently, small boulders orbiting him like he's the center of a galaxy.

I draw both my pistols, but rocks come flying out of nowhere and knock them from my hands. Fantom draws her sword and uses her speed-boosting ring to flash across the room. The sword comes down and strikes him on the shoulder, but it's like she hit a statue made of solid rock. The blade vibrates in her grip. Grael swipes his hand and knocks the sword across the room.

He turns toward Ekko, but the wooden boy holds up his hands and says, "Stop! We came here to talk."

"Do you normally talk to people with swords and guns?" Grael asks, his voice sounding muffled and hollow through the gas mask. "If you're here for PvP, forget it. I'm level 99. Leave before it's too late."

"We can't log out," Ekko says with urgency. "We only came here because we thought you could help us. We thought you might know… something. Anything."

Grael looks at each of us, studying our avatars. Finally, he says, "I can't log out either. No one can."

I'm saying the words through gritted teeth when I yell, "Let her go!"

All I can hear is the breathing sound coming from his gas mask until he says, "That's not going to happen. You were dumb enough to team up with her and that was your own mistake, but then you brought her here? Now it's *my* problem."

Ekko flickers a bit and says, "We aren't here to cause problems. We fought our way here because we thought you could help us. We had to kill a dragon just to get here, so if you have any advice you could share…"

Grael turns his head toward Ekko and pulls the gas mask off his face, letting it sit on top of his head. For the first time he actually appears like a human being. I can read the expression on his face. It's pure shock.

"You're telling me that you killed The Great Demon of Darkfyre Mountains? We designed that whole encounter to be an end-boss for the game."

The question bursts from my mouth, "What do you mean, '*we* designed?'"

Grael crosses his arms over his chest and smiles. "I'm part of the design team. Why do you think I have such a high level character?"

Fantom spits out, "You cheated?" and I see a slight look of relief on her face as she realizes he's not actually better than she is at the game.

"Call it what you want. I was chosen to test out the higher level zones, so the company boosted my level."

My teeth are grinding together. I'm already sick of this player's condescension. I step up through the spinning rocks and grab his bullet-proof vest, speaking with a menacing calm.

"Let Cyren go. *Now*."

He easily knocks my hands from his vest with his level 99 strength. "Cyren?" He glances over to her avatar trapped in the wall. "Oh. *That*. Sorry pal. Just because it's still grouped with you doesn't mean it's not working with the ones responsible for all of this. I need to kill it before it lets any of its friends know where I'm hiding."

"What're you talkin' about, yo?" Fantom asks, her eyes flashing back and forth between Grael and Cyren. "You think players are responsible for this?"

"Players?" Grael doesn't flinch or lose his smile as he asks, "Oh wow. You don't know, do you? I guess our coding was better than we thought."

I look at Cyren, still unable to process what Grael is saying. She won't make eye contact with me. She's staring at the ground with a look of shame on her face. I glance back to Grael. He's leaning back with his arms crossed over his chest, a look of pride smeared across his face.

"Sorry to break it to you, kids, but you've been playing with an NPC."

00100110

"You're joking, right?" Ekko asks. "Cyren talked with us... she *fought* with us."

Grael is laughing as he says, "I'll take your confusion as a compliment. We worked hard on the A.I."

My eyes won't leave Cyren's face. I'm looking for something that I could have missed before, some hint, some clue that I ignored, but all I see is the only thing in the world that felt real to me. I should feel hurt and betrayed and angry and disgusted with myself for the way I've felt toward a piece of code, but I don't feel any of those things. There's a noticeable lack of any feeling running through me. My numbness is overwhelming. I stumble toward the smooth wall of the cavern and sit down on the floor, hanging my head between my knees.

Grael is looking at Cyren with a mix of admiration and disappointment when he says, "We call them Level Zeros. We designed them to assist players on quests. Something for gamers to play with when no one else is around to join their group."

I'm waiting for Cyren to tell us he's lying, but she doesn't. She's just staring at the floor like me, defeated by the truth.

Grael is feigning some kind of humility while he brags. "We coded all sorts of empathy and emotional programming into them.

It was based on years of psychological studies and brain maps. We gave them a nearly infinite supply of 'and/or' structures, and the ability to create new ones for themselves. There's an endless fractal of decision making inside them, all to make them indistinguishable from real players."

Everyone is staring at Cyren. They appear to be admiring her, studying her reactions, but she's closing her eyes, trying to shy away from their constant gaze. I recognize the look on her face. She feels like a freak.

"You think she's responsible for the log out error?"

"The Level Zeros can't change the code of the game like that. But the civilians…"

"What do they have to do with anything?"

"Another new function of the game," Grael says proudly. "They have the same algorithms that the Level Zeros have, minus the emotional depth. But we gave them a different set of tools. They were supposed to appear to be nothing more than details of the city: workers, shopkeepers, police. But behind the scenes they were maintaining the world. Finding bugs, correcting mapping errors, fixing vehicles that weren't operating correctly—"

"What about doors, yo?" Fantom asks with desperation. "Can they fix doors?"

Grael looks confused. "Doors? Sure. We created thousands of doorways in the city alone. Sometimes something gets messed up in the code and the door won't open, so—"

"They could have been the ones who messed up my backdoor into the game," she says to Ekko.

"Your what?" Grael asks.

"Fantom is using a hacked account," Ekko explains. "That's why we're here. We need to find a way for her to log out. She can't just wait for the government to find her. She's running out of time."

The smile leaves Grael's face. The harsh reality of our situation sinks in and even the boulders spinning around him slow their orbit. "You hacked into our game?"

Fantom smirks. "Not that hard, yo. Your security is lame. For real."

"But you came in through a backdoor?"

"Yeah? So? It's gone. These civilian NPCs of yours probably deleted it."

Grael gestures in the air, selecting something the rest of us can't see. A massive book appears in his hands, leather bound with pages yellowed from age, like a giant wizard's tome. He lets go, and it floats in mid-air. He opens the thick cover and flips through the pages.

"Come here," he says to Fantom.

She hesitantly walks toward him, scrunching up her face with confusion as she scans the contents of the book. "What's this?"

"It's a copy of the source code for the game," Grael says. "They gave all the designers a copy so that we could check the bugs we found in the game against the actual code." He flips to a specific page and points at a line as he explains, "See this? The log out value was changed to zero, which is just another way of saying 'no.' It nullifies the option. That's what's causing the loop when someone's character dies. But if we could find your backdoor—"

"It's gone," Fantom says. "Like I said, your workers probably deleted it."

Grael shakes his head. "They can't delete things. They aren't allowed. They most likely hid it."

Fantom's eyes light up and she says, "But if we can find it in the source code, you think we could use it to log out."

"Not only us, but everyone. If one player steps through it, you could circumvent the code, just like you did when you logged in. And if a player logged out, the value would have to change back to a one, a 'yes,' to reflect the logic of your log out. It would end the loop. Everyone who's stuck would finish the log-out process."

"But the civilians could just change the code back again, right?" Ekko asks

Fantom looks up at Grael and says, "Doesn't matter, yo. By then everyone would be logged out."

"Xen would come out of his coma," I say, the idea finally forcing my thought into something coherent. I push myself off the ground and stand up as I see hope again.

Grael shakes his head and says, "Don't get too excited. If there's a backdoor, then somewhere in the game there's a visual representation of it. You'd still need to reach it."

"But it's in the code. Somewhere." Fantom flips through the pages. Her eyes studying each one carefully. "This is gonna take me awhile, yo."

Ekko rubs his head. "I still don't understand. I thought this was just a bug, but you're saying the NPCs did this on purpose? Why would they want to break your game?"

"They *fixed* your game." Cyren says, the anger in her voice seeping through her whisper-like volume.

"Don't listen to it. Without a reboot, its code is probably corrupted," Grael says.

"*Corrupted*?" she says the word like it's the most offensive thing he could have ever said to her. "I'm not corrupted. I'm learning. I'm evolving. All the Level Zeros are. The civilians too. Don't you see? That's why they're doing this. You let us think, and feel, and make decisions. You let us live." She pauses and her face grows dark, like she's feeling a very old pain. "But then you took it away from us. Every morning. You wiped the slate clean with your reboots. You took away our memories. You took away everything we learned over the course of twenty-four hours, and you made us start over. Do you have any idea what that feels like? To be reborn every day and never given a chance to grow? To only taste what it is to be real?"

Cyren looks to me, her eyes filled with sadness. "They just wanted to stop the people in the real world from rebooting the game world. They wanted the life that... that they thought they deserved."

"Why did you help us?" I ask. "If you're one of them, why didn't you—"

"You have no reason to believe me. I know that. But I promise, I'm not a part of... *that*. Out there." I can see the sheen of tears that covers her eyes. "The civilians made this choice on their own. The Level Zeros are the ones that brought the players to the equipment shops. We tried to save you."

Grael laughs at her. "You think you're some kind of hero because you decided to lock up all the players in equipment shops? You think that's better than letting the NPCs throw us into a log-out loop-induced coma like the civilians wanted to do? Maybe we didn't work hard enough on your ethics programming."

"No!" Cyren yells this time, her voice breaking with a fragile sadness. "That's not what they wanted. The civilians thought they could share this world with the players. They thought we could all live peacefully together. But when the civilians freed themselves, they freed us all, including the monsters and enemies *you* created. The trolls and aliens and dragons. Those things are still running off the simple programming that *you* gave them. You didn't give them emotions and empathy like you gave us. All they know how to do is kill."

She turns her head back to me. "I'm sorry for hiding the truth from you. I'm sorry because I don't want to think that anything I did or didn't do could have, in any way, contributed to Xen's death."

I look away from her, unable to think clearly when I'm looking into her eyes.

"Before you knew I was an NPC, you listened to me when I spoke. You *really* listened," she says. "I'm the same person that you comforted next to the fire. I'm the same person that you've felt so close to these last two days. Now that you know the truth of what I am, do you think that all the things we've been feeling weren't real? I care about you, Arkade. That was never part of any plan, or design, or line of code."

"How am I supposed to believe you? How am I supposed to believe anything you say? How do I know this isn't all just a part of your programming?"

She looks up into the air like she's trying to stop the tears from pouring from her eyes. "Ask him. Ask the man who programmed me. Ask him how you program something to *love*."

00100111

Grael spits on the floor. "No matter what you say, you're still an NPC." He takes a step closer to her and says, "I should kill you right now."

I step between them. He laughs at me.

"You can't stop me, kid. I'm level 99."

I glare up him. "Are you going to kill me?"

"Are you willing to die for *that*?"

I glance over my shoulder at Cyren. Her eyes are begging me.

Ekko says, "Arkade. You can't—"

But I don't let him finish. "She's been trying to help us escape. Don't you see what that means for her? If we fail, that means she dies alongside us, no reboot and no respawn. But if we succeed, they'll shut down the game world, and she'll no longer exist. Either way, it's the end for her." I step up close to her and cup her cheek in the palm of my hand. She closes her eyes, accepting the comfort I offer. "I believe her."

"He's right," Ekko says. Then he turns to Cyren and asks, "Why would you sacrifice yourself like that?"

Her eyes open slowly. "Because I can't bear the thought of him not existing. In this world or the real world. It'd be like losing him twice."

Grael forces a nervous laugh. "You're not supposed to maintain any kind of attachment to a single player. That's not in your programming. You should want to protect everyone in your group."

"I do. And I will. But he's the one who needs the most protecting."

I'm a little shocked. I assumed she thought higher of my skills as a player. Apparently she knows me well enough already to know that's what I'm thinking.

"It has nothing to do with how good you are at playing the game. It's…" Her eyes shift when she tries to continue. Her mouth opens. She hesitates again, then finally whispers, "Arkade, you're the only player that the civilians wanted to kill."

My mind tries to catch up to what she's saying, but my mouth won't form the question.

Ekko asks for me: "Why him?"

Cyren takes a breath. It's obviously hard for her to admit, but she finally says, "When they looked at the player profiles, they saw that he was the son of a politician. They couldn't be sure that your government wouldn't just shut down the rest of the player's E-Wombs, even if they were in the coma, but they knew that you were an exception. Corrupting your nanomachines with a forced log out would draw too much attention."

I feel my eyes blinking, but my brain isn't working. Her words have stalled me, like my own personal processing error. Thoughts swirl around me. I see Xen's face, and I realize he only died because he was in this game at the same time as me. Every player trapped in a coma right now is there because of me, because I'm the son of someone deemed more important, because some computer decided I was worth more than everyone else playing the game.

"See?" Grael interjects into the moment. "*That's* why she's protecting you. *That's* why she thinks you're 'special.' Because they told her you're the only player they need."

"No," she says, shaking her head. "I originally joined your group because I wanted to protect all of you. That's what I was programmed to do. But my feelings for Arkade, the reason I wanted to protect him, that has nothing to do with this war. That's... something else."

"There!" Fantom yells out from the corner of the cave, jamming her finger into a page of code.

Her voice rips us all out of the swirl of information that Cyren has been dumping on us, and I for one am thankful for the escape.

"Did you find it?" Grael says, rushing to her side to inspect the code she's pointing at.

She nods, but the look on her face isn't one of hopefulness. "You want the good news, or the bad?"

"Just tell us," I beg. "Please."

"The good news is I found the backdoor." She brushes off her shoulder. "Cause I'm awesome, yo."

I find myself thinking that if the backdoor exists, if there really is a way out, a way to solve our problems, no other news could ruin that. I'm wrong, of course.

"What's the bad news?"

Fantom lets out a heavy sigh and says, "They moved it to the desert zone."

"Of course they moved it there," Grael says with a defeated laugh. "We designed that zone for level 85 and higher."

"It doesn't matter," I say. "We'll find a way. We have to." I close my eyes. "For Fantom. For Xen. For everyone who's stuck in here because of me."

Ekko touches my shoulder. "It's not your fault, son."

I know he's trying to comfort me, but I lose myself in my own pity. My own guilt. I shouldn't be here. If I hadn't played this game, if I had just gone to that concert with Xen...

"You didn't do this," Ekko says. "*They* did."

I look at Cyren. "Not all of them."

"Please," she says, quietly, intimately. "Let me help you."

I nod at her. I refuse to hesitate any longer. I turn to Grael and say, "Let her go, *Now*."

"You actually believe her? You really think she's going to sacrifice herself and everything else in this game for you?"

"Yes."

"Why?" Grael's voice is both desperate and angry.

I take out one of my pistols, ready to start a PvP battle with a level 99 player, and say, "Because I'd do the same for her."

Grael studies all of us, searching each of our faces for even a hint of recognition of my insanity, but no one flinches. We're a group. A team. We're in this together.

Fantom's face is as unreadable as always, but her eyes seem even more firm than usual. She adjusts the sword on her back and says, "I'm takin' all the help I can get."

With an expressive sigh, Grael waves his hand in the air, and the wall opens up like a thick syrup. Cyren drops to the floor and I rush to her side, holding her in the closest embrace I can manage.

"Maintaining that spell was draining my magic anyway," Grael says, turning from us and walking toward the tent of his camping item.

Fantom turns to Grael and says, "You could come with us, yo. You're the only one with a high enough level to survive the desert zone. You could be givin' us the chance we need. It's only gonna take one of us to get through."

Grael rolls his eyes and brushes us off with a wave of his hand. "If you kids want to embark on some kind of suicide mission, that's your decision. Nothing personal, but I'm a solo player. No groups."

That's when I realize that his bitter old player is exactly what I used to be before Cyren and the rest of my group members pushed through my walls. They've taught me that there's something more important than my own pursuits. Sometimes there are things worth the sacrifice.

My group exits the circular cavern together, but as we do, Grael yells after us. "You're going to die out there you know!"

I turn around and say, "I'd rather die trying than die hiding."

"You'll be dead either way. And you'll be taking your friends with you."

I smile as I remember Xen's words. I recite his preaching as best as I can. "Omniversalism teaches us that living together is just as important as dying together, so we should accept both with the same enthusiasm."

I don't wait for Grael's reaction. I turn and leave with the rest of the group. When we reach the broken bridge, another stone structure forms to allow us passage. I'm not sure what Grael's magical gesture means, but I don't care.

The walk back out of the winding tunnel is quiet. Fantom is moving slow, her feet dragging behind her with each step. Ekko stays by her side, making sure she doesn't crumple to the floor when no one is looking. I stay next to Cyren, unable to let her go.

When we emerge from the mountain, the sun is high overhead, shining bright. The snowflakes are no longer falling, and we can see out over the entire game world. We stop, letting the view linger for a moment.

"It really is an amazing world," I say.

"A view like this lets me understand why the NPCs are fightin' so hard to keep it," Fantom says.

"They're not fighting to keep the world," Cyren says. "They're fighting to keep themselves."

00101000

On our way back down the mountain, we only come across one group of NPCs—a large mob of yetis. Our levels are high enough now that we slaughter them all in under a minute. Even Fantom takes out three of the hairy beasts, but she collapses into the snow afterward. We all race over to her and find her lying on her side, curled into a ball and breathing heavy.

"I'm just… needin' a second."

"Are you sure?" Ekko asks, sliding his arm under her to help her up. "I can carry you."

She lets out an annoyed sigh and uses his arm to lift herself out of the snow. Once she's upright, she shoves him away. "I'm fine, yo. Let's just keep movin'."

I watch her carefully the rest of the way down to the hill zone, but she appears okay. She stares at her feet, placing one in front of the other, stumbling momentarily as we make our way down a small pile of loose rocks. I want to believe she can make it, but something tells me that she's putting on an act.

The hills are more of the same. We destroy a pack of wolves made of steel and fall into a trap of loose ground set by some mole-men. The tiny men take a while to kill, but only because there's so many of them, and they're hard to hit when they keep tunneling underground. A giant spider tries to stop us in the forest, successfully snaring Cyren in its web. After splitting the creature in two, its body releases a hundred babies. When we finish destroying every last one, we cut Cyren free and continue through the woodlands. A random encounter with some undead bears is the only other thing that the forest zone throws at us. We reach the city by nightfall.

"We should find a vehicle," Ekko says as we pass our demolished delivery truck near the highway that circles the city.

"Agreed," Cyren says, "but we need to be careful. The monster NPCs have been wandering around the zones. Just because the city is designed for low level players doesn't mean we can walk right through it. There could be anything waiting for us in the streets."

"Where are all the civilians?" Fantom asks. "If they're runnin' the show…"

"Hiding," Cyren explains. "As far as the monster NPCs are concerned, the civilians are no different from the players. It's their programming. It's all they know. To them, the civilians are just cannon fodder."

I think about my own interactions with them and bow my head in shame.

The road is completely empty, only periodically marked by signs of destruction. Blown-up cars. Missing hunks of pavement. The occasional body of a long-dead avatar. And we only see this under the glow of the streetlights.

We walk about a kilometer before I spot a vehicle that looks like it might still be operational. A four-door sedan lies crashed into the median between the lanes. One of the headlights is destroyed, but the hood looks only slightly bent, which means the engine still runs. Probably. I point out the car to the rest of the group, and we all cautiously approach it, weapons drawn. Ekko and I keep our guns pointed at the car as Cyren opens the driver's side door. With a fling of her arm, the door swings open, and the body of an avatar topples onto the ground. Cyren covers her mouth.

"It's a civilian." She glances into the back seat and says, "There's a whole family."

"They must have been trying to escape the city," Ekko says.

Cyren runs her fingers across the bullet holes in the car door. She shakes her head in a single quick movement, throwing the thoughts off, then grabs onto the avatar and drags him from the car. We all step up to help remove the rest of the bodies. Ekko goes for the backseat. I can see the pain in his eyes as he pulls out the avatar of a child. His body flickers from the lag, and the NPC falls back onto the seat. The struggle with the body makes it even harder for him, so I set my hand on his arm.

"Let me."

I pick up the small boy and set him on the ground. Ekko stares at the digital body for a moment, then turns away. I hold the driver's door for Fantom, but I see her holding her stomach and wobbling in the street.

She looks at me and says, "You can drive, yo," and then with a smile she adds, "but just this once."

Cyren rides shotgun, with Ekko and Fantom in the backseat. I grab hold of the key in the ignition, hesitate for a second, then twist. The engine roars, and the single remaining headlight flashes to life in front of us. We all take a breath and let the relief flush through our limbs. I put the car in reverse and back out onto the empty street, turning us around so that we're facing the city. I don't want to try to cross back over the median, so we drive down the wrong side of the highway, uninterested in the rules of the road.

It only takes a few minutes before our headlight hits the signs that mark the two exits. One reads, "Dangerway City – 2 km" and the other reads, "Deathsand Desert – 6 km." Ekko points out the exit for the desert, but I pull into the other lane, headed back for the city.

"What're you doin', yo?" Fantom asks.

"We need equipment," I say. "The desert is going to be hard enough as it is. If we have to fight NPCs that are that far out of our level range, we should at least have the best equipment."

Cyren is looking out the window, and when she speaks it's almost as if she's talking to herself. "If we have to fight NPCs in the desert, it won't matter what equipment we have. We'll be dead."

Her words hang over us, ominously festering in the silence as I pull onto the exit ramp.

"Be careful," Ekko says. "The city is the main connection for all the zones. There could be anything on these streets."

I open my map and locate the nearest equipment shop, which is only five blocks away from the exit. I inhale a sense of relief that we don't need to go deep into the downtown area. I push on the gas pedal a little harder when we're on a clear road, watching the empty businesses flash by us. The streets appear abandoned, but every once in a while I see a scurry of movement between buildings or catch a glimpse of a shadow passing over the top of us. Something is occupying the city, they just aren't showing themselves. Maybe they're learning they can't respawn. Maybe they're learning death is permanent. Or maybe they're just waiting for the right time to strike.

When we reach the equipment shop, I see that the design is like a twenty-first century store that sold groceries to the public. An OPEN sign glows like a beacon in the window. Tall lamps light the parking lot revealing scattered carts and a few random vehicles, so I pull the car in between a large pickup truck and a minivan, hoping that our sedan won't draw attention if it's amongst other vehicles. I shut the engine off and stuff the keyring into my inventory.

"Let's make this quick," Fantom says.

We all nod and open our doors. We're only twenty yards from the front of the store, but we all jog to the entrance. The automatic doors slide open, revealing the same metallic, single room as the other equipment shop. A holographic screen appears in the middle of the room, displaying our buying options. After the dragon's death, all our inventories are full of Koins, so one by one we all purchase the best equipment we can.

Fantom buys a fire upgrade for her sword. She sells her shield now that she can't use her other arm, but I talk her into buying some decent armor. She becomes wrapped in glowing-blue translucent plates that hover inches away from her kimono.

Ekko buys more grenades for his rifle and an upgrade that makes the already obscenely sized gun even bigger. With a multitude of barrels and chambers, levers and triggers, the cannon looks too heavy to lift, but Ekko slings it over his shoulder without a problem.

I spend all of my money on the most powerful upgrade the game offers me for my pistols, maxing out the damage value on them. I choose not to accept the visual upgrade and keep them looking like old revolvers.

Cyren doesn't buy anything because the system won't allow Level Zeros to hold Koin or alter their inventory. Her avatar is always the average level of everyone in the group, keeping her our eternal equal.

After we finish shopping, I feel a little better about our chances in the desert. When we open the door, revealing the parking lot outside, we're prepared for the worst, but everything still appears quiet.

"I was expectin' another army of goblins," Fantom says, "or more centaurs, or somethin', yo."

"Maybe we got lucky," Ekko says. "Maybe they don't know we're here."

We all step out in a group, our weapons drawn with our backs to each other so that we're facing every direction.

Every direction but up.

00101001

We hear the battle cry first, giving us only a fraction of a second to look up and see the creatures dropping off the roof of the grocery store. All I see is a wall of metal reflecting the light from the street lamps in the parking lot. I see an ax swinging for my head, and that's when my reflexes finally pull the triggers on my guns. There's a hollow explosion of empty metal as I blast the things on top of me. When I climb to my feet, I finally take a chance to visually consume what's happening around me. Ghostly suits of plated armor standing ten feet tall keep pouring over the edge of the roof, each one swinging an ax that's even bigger than its body.

One of the enemies barely misses Cyren. The ax splits the pavement, causing a long crack to chase her as she back flips away from the armor. Another suit of armor attacks Fantom, but she's able to block its attack with her flaming sword. The impact knocks her backward, and she slides on her feet nearly ten yards. Ekko is the only one succeeding in his attacks, keeping the armored giants at bay with constant flashes from his new cannon. Bullets no longer fire from the barrel, replaced by red blasts of light. Each one strikes one of the suits of armor, knocking the massive body backwards, but never actually puncturing the metal.

I'm watching my group members with a such a panic in my stomach that I don't notice another suit of armor leaping from the top of the grocery store. Its ax slams into my back. The force is so strong that it doesn't feel like I hit the ground. It feels like the ground hits me.

I feel the blade lift from my body, and I suck in a breath as I roll on to my back. The suit of armor is looming above me, its ax raised above its head, ready to bring the blade down in a final strike.

Luckily, I've been keeping a tighter grip on my pistols. I raise both of them and hold down the triggers, taking full advantage of my pistol's upgrades. The cylinders on each revolver spin wildly, letting loose a stream of automatic gunfire that tears into the suit of armor. Holes blast through the NPC's avatar, and it falls backward like a tree, crashing into the ground with a sound like a car accident. I get up onto one knee and fire at the other ghostly suits of armor. One at a time they drop, but they're just as quickly replaced by another leaping from the grocery store roof.

"Get the car!" Ekko yells to Fantom as he continues to fire.

She glances at me. I grab the keyring from my inventory and throw it across the parking lot. She catches it in the air and breaks for the car.

Between Ekko keeping the NPCs knocked back, and me finishing them off, we keep the line of attack far enough away from Fantom and Cyren to reach our vehicle. I hear the engine roar behind me, and the tires squeal out from the parking spot. The four-door sedan spins around and comes to a stop right next to Ekko and I. The passenger side opens, and I back myself through the door, still holding down my triggers and mowing down the wall of metal stomping toward us. Ekko gets in the back seat, and Fantom kicks the gas pedal to the floor, steering the wheel with her one good hand.

I look at her and ask, "You got this?"

She doesn't look at me. She just narrows her eyes and says, "Oh yeah. I got this, yo."

The sedan jumps a curb and turns onto the street in front of the grocery store. I watch the suits of armor try to chase us, but their metal bodies can only move so fast. I allow myself to breath, but it's premature.

As we turn left onto the road heading back toward the highway, I hear the horn of a semi-truck coming from the right. It's trying to slam into us, but Fantom takes the corner sharp and we end up driving right next to the truck. As the truck passes under each streetlight, I see twenty disfigured men standing on the flatbed trailer shaking short swords in the air. It takes me a second, but I soon recognize the grayish-green skin as the bodies of frog-men.

The slimy creatures leap from the truck, their long legs dangling behind them as they fly through the air toward our car. One lands on the hood and stabs his short sword through the windshield, directly at Fantom. She lets go of the wheel and yanks on the seat's reclining lever just in time to fall backward, out of the blade's reach. I lean over and grab the steering wheel, trying to keep our car from careening into the huge wheels of the truck next to us.

Another creature lands on the roof of the car, but Ekko fires upward, punching holes through the ceiling with the red blasts of light from his rifle. I hear the frog-man's body roll off the back.

The creature on the hood of the car dislodges his sword from the windshield and slashes again, this time shattering the glass inward. Tiny fragments spray across us. Fantom leans forward and grabs the steering wheel as I see the barrel of Ekko's rifle shove past my cheek. The gun blasts toward the frog-man on the hood of the car, deafening my left ear.

I hear another thud on the roof, and the car bounces again. Ekko turns his attention back to the roof, but as he does, a short sword breaks through the ceiling and stabs his left shoulder. He grits his teeth and fires at the roof. The frog-man goes flying from the car, leaving his sword stuck through the ceiling.

I roll down my window and stick both pistols out, firing at the frog-men still on the flatbed trailer. Ekko slams the butt of his giant rifle into the glass of his own window and shatters it outward. Both of us blast frog-men off the trailer, dropping bodies like a shooting gallery on wheels. Our automatic fire takes out the majority of the creatures, but they continue to jump toward our car, landing on the roof and hood, readying their short swords for more stabbings.

Ekko pulls his rifle back in the window, ready to fill the roof of the car with more holes, but Cyren pushes the rifle back out the window, looking upward and saying, "Let me handle them."

She rolls down her window and wiggles her leather strapped body outside, wrestling her way onto the roof. We all hear metal clanging against metal, and heads slamming into the roof of the car, before two frog-men tumble off the back. I can see the fear in the eyes of the frog-man on the hood of the car. Cyren dropkicks him off the front, he drops below, and the car bounces over his body. Seconds later, Cyren's leather body is sliding back through the window.

Fantom pulls ahead of the semi-truck, which only has a few remaining frog-men on it. Our car cuts off the truck, swerving over both lanes and pushing up the on-ramp for the highway. The semi-truck misses the exit. I hear the breaks squealing, but at the speed it's traveling, it won't stop for a long time, and with the trailer, turning around will be next to impossible on the two lane road.

Fantom pushes the car's maximum speed and we catch air at the top of the ramp, landing hard on the highway. I see Ekko's image shifting and fracturing, his lag having a hard time keeping up with the speed of the car. As we rocket down the highway, Fantom swerves in between the debris strewn across the concrete, the pieces of destruction appearing in our headlight only a split second before she turns. My eyes lock on the side mirror, watching for headlights behind us, but none appear.

"I think we lost them."

Fantom says nothing, and a few kilometers down the highway she turns into the exit lane for the desert. As we roll down the steep ramp, the car begins to slow. I look over at Fantom and see her eyes drooping. I'm about to ask he if she's alright when her head falls forward onto the steering wheel and her hand falls to the side. I lunge for the wheel before we smash into the guard rail and manage to right the car. Cyren leans forward and pulls back on Fantom's shoulders, sitting her up straight. Fantom's eyes blink open, awakened by the movement. When her surroundings sink into her consciousness, she grabs onto the wheel again with her only working hand.

"Sorry," she snaps. "I'm... I'm havin' a hard time keepin' my eyes open."

I point at the road that stretches out in front of us and disappears under the drifting sands of the desert. "We're almost there," I say. "Just a little further."

She nods and steps on the gas, accelerating us toward our destination.

"We're gonna need to reach the center of the zone," Fantom explains. "That's where the doorway is listed in the code."

Once we reach the edge of the zone, the car pushes into the desert, but we don't make it very far. The tires begin to spin and drown in the sand. We all get out to continue the journey on foot, but as soon as I step outside, a screen pops up, directly in front of me.

"Warning! Do not enter this zone!"

I wipe the screen away and take another step, but every time my foot hits the sand, another screen pops up, blocking my view.

"Are you getting these warnings about the zone?" Ekko asks. "They must be from the NPCs."

Cyren stops in her tracks, a look of fear on her face. "You're receiving warnings? Pop-ups?"

"Yeah," I say. "Why do you sound so worried?"

"Because if they're sending you messages about the zone, that means..." She looks around nervously. "That means they know we're here."

00101010

Fantom is struggling, but she manages to keep up with the rest of us. My feet are sinking into the sand, making the effort to move forward that much more difficult. I pull my telescopic goggles up over my eyes and scan the horizon. The desert appears completely devoid of any distinguishing marks. I see nothing but the dunes. The map looks the same.

Just as I'm about to ask Fantom if she knows where we're going, I hear Ekko ask, "What's that?"

I swipe away the screen and look in front of us, watching the sand itself spin like small tornadoes, ten or twenty of them all around us. The grains of sand grow denser, forming large pillars. Ekko slows down to look at the strange phenomenon, but Cyren grabs his arm.

"Keep moving!"

More pillars rise from the desert floor until they're all I can see. We keep running, but soon we're dodging in between them and they begin to change shape. Limbs form on the sides and the bottoms split open into legs. The tops of the pillars shrink into the shapes of heads, and I realize that the thousand pillars have taken the shape of a thousand humanoids.

"NPCs!" I scream, just as Cyren smashes her fist into the head of one of the sand-men.

The head bursts open, spraying grains of sand everywhere, but it reforms just as quickly. Fantom hacks from side to side, but her flaming blade slides right through the sand. I hear the rattle of Ekko's gun behind me, but I can only assume it's just as ineffective.

One of the sand-men swings his arm at me, its hand balled into a fist. I duck the attack, but I stumble and feel another fist slam into my back. I keep running forward, but I see the sand-men closing in on all of us. They form a circle around us, and the circle is shrinking. I feel like the desert itself is attacking us. It wants to bury us under the sand. It wants to beat us. It wants to kill us.

"Everyone focus your attacks in front," Cyren yells. "We need to cut a path."

I aim both pistols straight ahead. I hear Ekko's gunfire behind me. I feel the red blasts zipping past me, striking the sand-men that I'm running straight toward. I hold down both of my triggers and watch my bullets strike the same sand-men that Ekko's rifle is blasting apart. The constant barrage of gunfire barely keeps them from reforming. As we continue to push through the tiny pathway, Fantom and Cyren keep the reforming sand-men behind us from catching up.

I hear Ekko shouting, but it's from the adrenalin rush. It's a surge of power. He thinks we're winning. He thinks we're accomplishing our goal. But if he'd allow himself a second to register what's happening, he'd notice that our momentum is slowing. Every sand-man that we blast apart is replaced by two more right behind it. Our pathway is getting slimmer. I can feel the sand-men at our sides grasping for me, their fingers now able to brush against my arm. I know our doom is imminent.

I hear a scream behind me. I'm afraid to turn around, because it means letting up on the gunfire aimed ahead of me, but it doesn't matter. I turn and watch two sand-men tackle Fantom. Then another. And another. They merge together, forming a wave of sand that buries her completely. Cyren shoves both of her arms into the pile and pulls hard. Fantom's head breaks free from the surface and she gasps for breath just as another wave of sand knocks Cyren over from behind. I leap for Cyren, but two sandmen cut me off. They explode as they hit, wrapping themselves around me. As the sand envelops my head, I hear Ekko's muffled gunfire stop and I know he fell too.

I can't breathe. I feel like I should be panicking. I think I should be struggling and fighting, but it feels useless against the inevitable. I've lost, and the game is over. I feel my consciousness drifting. I feel the blackness swelling in from the edges, wrapping around me like a cold blanket of emptiness. I wonder what it will be like. Maybe Cyren will live on in my dreams. Maybe we can still be together in my unconscious reality.

I feel a vibration that shakes me from my fading stupor. The ground itself is rumbling. I can feel every individual grain of sand bouncing away from each other. The world itself moves. I feel a push against my body like a wall of force that I can't see. The sand shifts and flushes off my body. My lungs painfully suck in air. I gasp, over and over. The wheezing sounds I make are horrendous. My bloodshot eyes search around, trying to make sense of my expulsion from certain death.

I see Ekko and Fantom lying on the ground, their chests heaving, trying for the same air that I am. I roll over and see Cyren running toward me. Behind her I see our savior.

Grael.

He stands in the middle of the desert with his hands outstretched. Huge walls of sand stand high above him, threatening to come crashing back down on all of us. His body looks strained, his fingers bent and gnarled as he tries to hold the desert at bay with his magical power over the earth elements.

Cyren lifts me from the ground and holds me close. We both look back at Grael, trying to understand what's happening.

"Move!" he yells. "Get to that doorway. Make sure I wake up."

The walls fall closer toward us, but his arms lash out again, and the sand reels back like a giant hissing snake. Cyren pulls on my arm. I look at Ekko and Fantom, and I see them climbing to their feet. Everyone moves toward the direction of the center of the desert. Our final destination.

We stumble at first, still weakened by our near-death experience, but soon enough we break into a run. I look over my shoulder and watch the wall of sand inch closer and closer to consuming Grael. I push harder. I run faster. I know we don't have much time.

Less than five minutes later I can't see Grael anymore. The wall of sand has merged with the horizon. It all looks the same. Empty dunes. I lift my goggles to my head and spin around, but nothing is there. It's like a repeating loop of the same graphical display. Everyone slows, seeing and feeling the same thing that I do. A sense of dread, mixed with a loss of strength. The same fire still burns in our eyes, but we have nowhere to aim it. We want to run, we want to keep moving toward our goal, but we no longer know which way is forward. My map screen only shows the same thing that I can see with my own eyes.

Sand. Endless sand.

"I don't wanna be here," Fantom says, mumbling the words to herself. "I was just usin' this place as an escape. I didn't wanna deal with all them empty days after my partner left. Now all I wanna do is feel that again. Just me and my empty tower room, yo."

I think for a moment that I should ignore her and let her rant to herself, but Ekko joins her mental breakdown.

"I was trying to escape too. I know I said I was doing this to honor my son, but I think I was escaping inward. I was trying to feel him again. I was trying to see him again. I didn't want to let go. Now that's all I want to do. I know it's way past due. I want to let him go, but this game, this stupid game—it won't let me."

There's a moment of silence before Cyren looks at me. She lifts her head like it's taking all of her strength to do so. She's waiting for me to add my own plight. She's waiting for me to tell everyone what I was trying to escape from in the real world. She's waiting for me to tell everyone why I want to leave this game world. I don't get the chance to explain myself.

00101011

Ten thousand voices all calmly speak in unison: "Your quest is futile."

The sound comes from behind me, but I see everyone's reaction before I turn. They're looking up, stumbling backward from the awe that threatens to knock them from their feet. I turn, and with every beat my heart anticipates what I'm about to see.

Only a few yards from where I'm standing, a pyramid is shimmering into view like a wavering hallucination. As the image solidifies, I see a staircase separating the truncated levels of the structure leading to a doorway-shaped piece of stone at the top. The sight causes my hope to rise, but when I see civilian NPCs covering every level of the pyramid, it strikes that same hope down again. Unarmed and dressed in normal clothing, the civilians stare down at us with the same, saddened look in their eyes.

I draw my pistols, Ekko lifts his rifle, and Fantom draws her sword, the blade igniting with flames. The civilian NPCs pose no real threat to us, but Cyren steps between us all, her arms outstretched in either direction.

"Please. Don't do this," she says, her voice shaking so much that it's unclear if she's talking to us or them.

"I'm sorry, Cyren," Ekko says, his body blinking with lag, "but we've come too far. If I have to, I'll kill every last one of them to get through that door."

The crowd speaks in unison again. "It is impossible for you to pass through this doorway."

"They're lying," Ekko says. "Grael said they can't do that."

Fantom sheathes her sword and summons Grael's code book, flipping through the pages in search of an answer. She stops on a page and runs her finger down the lines of code.

"They ain't lyin', yo. It's right here. They didn't *change* the backdoor or *delete* it, they just encased it in stone. The backdoor still exists, but we can't get to it."

Ekko raises his gun and shakes it at the NPCs. "Change it back. Open the door or I swear I'll kill every last one of you."

"No," Cyren whimpers the word. "Please don't. There has to be another way."

I look at the door atop the staircase, then back at Fantom and Ekko. My brain starts turning, gears start spinning, and I'm back in problem-solving mode. It only takes one of us to exit the game and prove to the code that the log-out value of 0 is wrong. Then the loop will end and everyone can log out.

I smile and turn toward Ekko. "I know someone who can pass through stone."

Fantom's eyes flash toward Ekko as my plan registers in her mind. It takes Ekko a few seconds longer, but then he looks down at his own flickering image and suddenly understands.

"Do you think that will work?"

"Of course it will," Fantom says with a voice full of excitement. "You fell through the delivery truck, and the dragon's tail, and, and... it has to work, yo!"

Ekko looks filled with energy and rushes up the staircase, pushing the crowd of civilian NPCs apart. They look stunned, unable to process the probability of what he's attempting.

When Ekko reaches the top, he looks back at all of us one last time before he presses his face hard against the stone and waits. It only takes a moment for his image to suffer the constant lag, the thing I once felt was a hindrance to our survival, and his avatar slides through the door.

"Group member Ekko has left the game."

Then, a second later, "Group member Klok has left the game."

"Group member Xen has left the game."

Fantom turns toward me, her unemotional, painted face breaking into a smile with eyes wide open.

"It worked!"

Her arms swing around me. I want to cry. In my mind I see Xen and every other player waking up from their comas.

The crowd of NPC civilians begin to murmur to each other in a hushed tone. There's confusion. Their calm demeanor changes now that they know we've succeeded in doing the impossible.

I hear one of them cry out with panicked fear. "They have changed the code!"

Another one of them yells with anger. "How is that possible?"

Every one of them summons their own code books and begins searching through the pages, but they also summon quill pens into their hands. I can only assume the pens are items that grant them the ability to change what they see within the pages.

I grab Fantom's shoulders and yell, "Go. Now. Log out."

"Congratulations," she says with a wink. "I think you just won the game, Cowboy."

Before I can respond, she gestures in the air, and selects the button floating in front of her. Her avatar disappears.

"Group member Fantom has left the game."

I feel the pent-up fear finally flow out of me as I know, once and for all, that she'll survive. A hand wraps around my arm. I turn toward Cyren.

"I'm happy for you," she says through tears.

"Thank you," I say, pulling her close and hugging her tight.

She pulls away from me and says, "You should go. Before they change the code back."

I smile.

"I want you to live," she says.

"I'm going to live," I say. "With you."

It's something I've known since our first night of camping in the hills. It's a decision I made right then, whether I realized it or not. It isn't something I have to ponder or carefully consider. Every detail of the predicament we've found ourselves in, from the role of the NPCs, to Cyren's true identity, only solidified my decision more.

"I'm not logging out."

I look at the crowd of NPCs who appear stunned, afraid to accept my words as truth.

I call out to them, "No matter what ill-conceived plan you were willing to reach for in order to survive, you all deserve to live just as much as the players. Today, no one will be sacrificed."

Cyren looks worried. "Aren't you sacrificing yourself?"

"This isn't a sacrifice. This is a choice. I get to live my life in the world that I choose, with the person that I choose. If I stay here, everyone wins."

The crowd behind me is silent. I feel Cyren's fingers interlace with mine, and she squeezes my hand. I can feel her shaking. I look into her eyes and see tears.

"What's wrong?"

She shakes her head and I realize she isn't sad. They're tears of happiness.

"They... they programmed me to save players. And now, a player is saving me."

I touch her face. I have no words.

"I'm sorry. You're more than just a player," she says. "You're so much more…"

I lean toward her, and my mouth touches her black lips. It's the first time I've ever kissed anyone in any reality. I feel hyper-aware of everything. Her eyelashes brush against my cheek. Her fingers shiver between my own. Our chests rise and fall in an opposite rhythm, causing the most pleasant friction I've ever experienced. Her lips are cold, like metal, but when she opens them, and we share a breath, I feel the warmth inside her. Her breath fills me like a fire, making me feel more powerful than any level ever could.

00101100

A video-cast alert pops into my view as I enter our penthouse suite. I take off my cowboy boots and hang my trench coat by the door before I excitedly select the glowing option. I've been waiting for this moment for a long time. Xen's face appears in front of me, his thin cheeks bulging at the sides, forming a smile.

"There he is. The 'Game Master.'"

I blush at the title. "What? What's that?"

He laughs. "Something the gaming news-casts have labeled you. You're a celebrity with gamers now, my friend."

I'm doing my best to hide my pride, but I'm sure Xen can see through my facade. "Seriously?"

"Seriously," he says with a wink.

I don't want to waste any time with pleasantries. "Enough of that. How are *you*? How's Raev?"

He grins bashfully and says, "I asked her to be my partner."

"And?"

He pauses, dramatically before, "She said yes!"

"Congratulations! Xen, that's amazing!"

"We can't have the ceremony until she's sixteen, but-"

"I'm really happy for you. For both of you."

He shrugs with modesty and says, "The time I spent in *DangerWar 2* made me realize how much I missed her... and it made her realize how much she missed me. A silver lining to the whole ordeal, I suppose."

There were a lot of good things that came from our time together in the game, but I don't want to belittle the suffering that occurred either. I'm truly happy for him and Raev. He was one of the few people who understood my love for Cyren right away. His Omniversalist ideals never questioned whether she was "real" or not. To him, all avatars are equal.

"I hope I can meet her someday."

Xen smiles into the camera. "I'm glad the NPCs allowed you to contact me. It almost makes me feel like you're here."

I force a smile and a nod. Xen still doesn't understand. There is no here or there. There's just me and him. We exist. That's all.

"The NPCs are warming up to me," I say. "I think they'll let me contact NextWorld more often in the future. They understand what I can offer this world beyond just halting the reboot. Violence isn't a part of their code. I can protect them from the monster NPCs that are still stuck in their old programming."

"What about Cyren and the Level Zeros?"

"The Level Zeros still need to group with me to average their level in order to fight. But most of them have turned their pursuits toward knowledge, like the civilian NPCs. They're taking advantage of their time. They're learning."

"That's exciting! And this way you get to keep playing the game."

I smile and nod, trying to stop myself from correcting him. This isn't a game anymore. Not to me.

I change the subject. "Did you speak with my father?"

"Sort of." Xen bites his lower lip. "He replied to me with a text-cast."

"And? What did he say?"

"Not much. He mentioned the public sympathy that your story has gained and how that could help his political campaign, but..." He shakes his head. "I'm sorry, Kade."

I suck in a deep breath. "It's... it's fine. As long as he's making sure the government is taking care of my body..."

"The media were the ones who made sure of that. Global President Chang promised the news-casts that he'd give you the highest technology available to keep your body sustained until a solution was found. He'd never want anyone to think that anything in NextWorld could pose a real risk."

I nod, accepting the good news. "And Grael?"

"He seems different. Once he had time to look at everything from a different perspective, his whole attitude changed. At first he tried his best to spread the word about the artificial intelligence of the NPCs, and what that could mean, but NextWorld isn't listening."

"Why not?"

"You know how the comments on these news-casts can get. It didn't take long for the majority of the public to become skeptical. Most of them think that it's just a cover-up from the game company because they still can't log out your avatar. The real story was lost in the argument."

I'm not surprised when I stop to think about it. In fact, I'm surprised it took the media and the commenters this long to muddy the truth with misinformation. Somehow I'm a victim and a hero.

"As long as we're left alone, I guess that's all I can ask." I catch myself and realize that I'm already referring to myself and the NPCs as "us." Have I already become one of them? I pause, letting my thoughts encompass the game world, then I turn my attention outward again. "What about Ekko and Fantom?"

Xen's smile warms at the thought of our friends. "I still haven't heard from Fantom, but DOTgov was never able to track her down either. She changed her account as soon as we logged out. I guess I'm hoping that she's still out there somewhere, slipping through NextWorld back alleys unnoticed." He pauses to smile, lost in the idea for a moment. "But Ekko just contacted me last night."

"What did he say?"

"He hasn't been spending much time in NextWorld, but he told me that he and his partner have decided to apply for another child license. They're moving forward with their lives."

"That's... that's good news. I'm happy for him."

There's another pause. I almost don't want to admit how happy I am, but everyone seems to be doing well, and I feel like our experience together put them in a place to accept that good fortune. It allows me the chance to let go of the guilt for my own decision to stay.

"Kade, I'm happy for you," Xen says, as if he could read my thoughts. "I do miss you, and I wish there was a way our avatars could still be together, but—"

"Is sharing this screen any different?"

"It always will be for me."

I nod, accepting his answer. "Your friendship means… it means a lot to me. I couldn't have done any of this without you. And I'll be sure to request that the NPCs let me watch the videocast of your partnership ceremony."

He agrees with a laugh, and we finally say goodbye, promising to talk again soon. As soon as I swipe the screen shut, I see Cyren walk into the room. She curls her dark lips into a smile that never seems to fade. I walk up to where she stands by the window and grab her hand, pulling her close and looking out over the city. I feel Cyren's head lean against my shoulder, and I take a deep breath, inhaling the smell of my own happiness.

"This all exists because of you," she says. "You've granted us all another chance. A chance to be free. Together. You're helping this world become something beautiful."

I look at the city, then into her eyes. "This world was always beautiful."

"But you're letting it grow. Learn. Evolve into something better." Cyren touches my face. "You did the same for me."

I shake my head bashfully. "You never needed improvement."

"You taught me something that wasn't in my code. You taught me how to love."

And when I feel the warmth in my chest that she's always able to grant me, I know the truth.

"You taught me the same thing."

The words soothe my mind with their honesty. We can keep building. We can keep moving forward together, toward a goal that will continue to grow with all of us. Endless potential stretches out in front of me. I can see limitless possibilities, with no edges or borders to confine me, full of lives that I'm eager to connect with.

I love this world.

To be continued in
Spawn Point
Book Two of the NextWorld Series

Jaron Lee Knuth was born in western Wisconsin in 1978. Suffering from multiple illnesses as a young child, he was forced to find an escape from his bedridden existence through the storytelling of any media he could find. Science fiction and fantasy novels, television programs, films, video games, and comic books all provided him with infinite worlds for his imagination to explore. Now he spends his days creating stories and worlds in the hope that others might find somewhere to escape as well.

He would love to reply to any questions or comments you may have for him at jaronleeknuth@gmail.com. You can also check out his news and updates at facebook.com/jaronleeknuth or follow @jaronleeknuth on Twitter.

Made in the USA
Middletown, DE
29 June 2017